RISING RESISTANCE

GRAND HUMAN EMPIRE
BOOK 5

JOHN WILKER

Rogue Publishing

ISBN: 978-1-951964-33-7

Remember.
The yellow yak, flies a purple 747.
Chili fries ALWAYS come with a coke.

IYKYK...

CONTENTS

You're about to embark on another fun adventure!
The crew of the *Osprey* is at it again!

When you're done reading, I hope you'll take a minute to
leave a review!

It all started when Jackson "Jax" Caruso was hired by a mysterious businessman to rob a supply train. After forming a heist crew of old friends (the brothers Delphino), an ex-girlfriend (Kori Lightning), and a stranger with weird abilities, he realized they were working for the bad guys.

Doing the right thing sometimes comes at a cost.

Since then, it's been one major or minor catastrophe after another. From stealing data from the Imperial Science Directorate to uncovering one of the biggest mysteries in recent history—the location of the Ghost Fleet—Jax and Naomi always seem to be neck deep in something.

After getting themselves mixed up in the underhanded doings of one of the Empire's largest corporations, the pair are keeping a low profile on Kelso station until the heat dies down. If it dies down.

PROLOGUE

The alarm's gentle melody rose in volume until finally too loud to ignore. Kori Lightning rolled over and slapped at the screen of her gPhone charging on the nightstand. Finally, the tune stopped.

Rising from bed, she looked around. Her boss paid well enough that her quarters were what some might consider spacious, at least as far as space station lodgings went. After all, the bedroom was its own distinct room; that alone put her place in the top forty percent of nice quarters on Jericho station.

Padding to the head, she tapped her phone a few times to start her morning routine. Music with a heavy bass line started thumping throughout the space, and the coffeemaker in the small kitchenette started hissing and burbling. She sang along. "Gotta say it was a good day."

Stepping out the hatch into the narrow corridor of her residential section, she turned right. Her employer had an office suite in Sphere Two in what passed for the upscale section of Jericho station's business district. She lived in Sphere One, so it was a pleasant walk to start her day.

She made less than fifty feet when the lighting in the corridor flicked from sterile white to a deep red. The overhead speakers crackled. "Attention station residents. Imperial forces have arrived near the station." The message repeated, but offered no further details.

Kori swore and started to run. Her boss would want her nearby if the Imps were going to board the station. She had a lot of ground to cover. She made it another hundred meters before the lights flickered and another split second before the deck shook under her feet. This time, the speakers didn't make an announcement. They squawked an alert klaxon.

"What are you imperial assholes doing?" she mumbled to herself, stabbing the call button for the lift at the end of the corridor. By now, almost every hatch in the corridor was open.

"Hey! What's going on?" a man shouted from several doors away. Kori turned, but another head popped out of a door to reply. "Imps are firing on the station!" The deck shook again, more forcefully than before. Opening fire on the station made no sense. She shook her head.

The lift doors slid apart. Kori eyed the empty car before turning for the hatch that led to the survival stairs. She grabbed her gPhone, tapping the icon for her office. The stairs were already full of people when she stepped into the reinforced stairwell. The call was taking longer than usual to connect. She closed the communication app and pocketed her gPhone.

Jericho station's shape, two large spheres with a thick connecting structure, meant she'd need to change stairwells at least three, maybe four times and walk nearly a kilometer to the other sphere, to get to the office. The main beam was where much of the governmental and commercial spaces were located.

After changing stairwells once, Kori pulled out her gPhone again, tapping an icon. This time the call connected like normal. "It's Kori. What's going on?"

Her boss, Alfonse Cotto, sounded haggard. "We're packing what we can. Where are you? I've got the ship doing preflight checks now."

"On my way. About to enter the Span." She used the given name of the kilometer-long, thick connecting structure between the two spheres.

"Okay, hurr—" The call dropped into static then went silent.

Looking at her gPhone, she swore again. "No signal? Are you kidding me?" She continued to shove her way through the mass of people trying to go up and down the stairs, once again slipping her gPhone into her pocket. She had three levels to go before reaching a deck that connected to the Span.

Jericho station, like most independent space stations, had minimal defensive capabilities. The original agreement with the Emperor forbade such armaments. That didn't mean that many stations, Jericho included, didn't have plenty of unpublicized improvements.

Panels all around the two spheres and along the main central Span slid open to reveal starship-grade blaster turrets. The guns tracked, locking onto the nearest Imperial ship.

The three massive Adjudicator class battlecruisers had arrayed themselves around the station, their half-kilometer-diameter, mushroom-cap-shaped forward sections aimed at the station. Heavy blasters arrayed in multiple concentric circles around the forward section fired in fits and starts at the station, targeting the defensive batteries and communication arrays.

The station's shields were no match for the powerful Imperial blaster cannons brought to bear against them. With each impact, the shields flared orange and white.

What Jericho's weapons lacked in power, they made up for in quantity. Energy weapons lancing back and forth lit the space between the station and attacking ships like a star going nova.

On the bridge of the Imperial warship *Resolute*, Sub-Commander Pettit looked at the ship's commander, Josephine Chen. "Commander, the station governor is still ignoring our calls," she said.

The short-statured woman turned from the console she was studying. "Then we continue to pick the thorns off. These Indie stations have gotten far too used to lax Imperial oversight. If Jericho has to be an example, so be it. Oh. We should call in the Barricades, as well. We will stamp out whatever Resistance elements exist on this station."

"Yes, ma'am." The Sub-Commander nodded. Turning to the tactical station, she said, "Continue bombardment." Then to the communications officer, "Hail the second wave." The officer nodded.

The main thoroughfare that ran from Sphere One to Sphere Two and was home to much of Jericho's retail space was an absolute mess. Hundreds, if not thousands, of station residents were pushing in every direction, trying to get into and out of the Promenade to the various docking bays in the two spherical sections.

Kori's gPhone vibrated in her pocket. Hoping for a message from her employer, she saw it was a station wide alert. *Take shelter,* was all it said. Such an alert could be sent as a mesh alert, device to device.

Looking left and right, she did some quick mental math. She was still closer to Sphere One, where her quarters were. It was also where her boss kept an off-the-books personal yacht parked in one of the lower-level docking bays. He, his office, and whichever of her coworkers had made it to the office and his larger ship, were all in Sphere Two. She'd never make it.

She turned back toward Sphere One, pushing her way through the crowd with more urgency. The station might be telling people to take shelter—which, if the Promenade was an indicator, no one was doing—but she knew that once the station realized fighting was pointless and surrendered, shock troops would be next. The Empire would pacify the station by whatever means necessary.

Outside the station, a Barricade class interdiction cruiser dropped out of a wormhole. Three corvettes flanked it. The larger ship held back, powering up its powerful gravity wave generators. After humanity reverse engineered the FTL system of the Ganymede ship, it hadn't taken long to also figure out how to pull ships out of wormholes. It wasn't until the Empire formed that the technology was weaponized in the form of Barricade class cruisers.

The corvettes accelerated toward Jericho. The station's remaining defensive guns fired, concentrating on the closest corvette. Despite the efforts of the larger warships, the station still had enough weapons to pierce the smaller ship's shields. The explosion rocked the station.

Aboard the *Resolute*, Commander Chen growled. "Increase fire. I want every weapon emplacement on that station slagged."

"Aye, ma'am," someone in the tactical section replied.

She watched as fire from her ship and the other two Adjudicator class ships increased. Explosions rocked the station. The remaining corvettes could approach mostly unmolested.

"Imperial ships docking in Sphere Two," came over the station's loudspeakers. Kori stepped into a secondary docking bay where her destination sat on stubby landing gear. She thanked the Gods she didn't believe in that the ship was still there. She added a thanks that this particular bay wasn't packed with panicked station residents, yet.

The yacht's preflight took almost no time to complete. Her boss kept the small ship in a ready state, just in case. She hoped he and the rest of the employees made it to the main docking bay on Sphere One before the Imperials got there.

She powered up the lift engines and guided the small craft out of the bay. "Shit!" She pulled the flight controls hard over, narrowly avoiding a larger modified cargo hauler that was burning hard, hugging the station's hull.

Glancing out the forward window, she swore again. She was directly in the path of the interdictor, off in the distance. She adjusted her course to follow the ship that almost ran her down, putting the station between her and the large wormhole destabilizing cruiser.

Local space was a chaotic mess of ships large and small, all trying to flee. She saw an Imperial corvette approaching the main docking bay in Sphere Two while two more corvettes further out were using grapplers to detain any ship that got too close.

She watched as the wormhole generator spun up, tapping the fingers of her free hand on the console, waiting for the light to turn green. As far as the ship's meager sensors could tell, the interdictor hadn't yet powered up its powerful gravity wave generators.

The light on the console turned green, and she slapped the button next to it. Directly ahead, an orange-green-purple bruise in space appeared before opening up into a wormhole.

"I hope Jax is home," she said, slumping in the pilot's seat.

PART 1

CHAPTER 1

"I smell like burned wire," Naomi complained. She sat her glass down and looked at the remains of her lunch. "This sucks."

Jax took a long swallow of his own drink, glad Lucas finally restocked New Terra Lager. "Help the skinny weirdo, she said. It's the right thing to do, she said," Jax said in a nasally voice meant to mimic Naomi.

She glared. "It was the right thing to do. And I don't sound like that."

"And this is the reward." Jax shrugged and took a bite of his burger. "Helping station engineering make repairs for bargain basement wages because we have to lie low on account of being at the top of a mega-corp's shit list." He turned. "A mega-corp with deep pockets and a grudge."

Lucas slowed as he approached the pair. "You two good?"

Jax nodded. "Yeah, no time for a second round."

The cybernetically enhanced bartender returned the nod and continued down the length of the bar, checking in on folks. The lunch hour packed the Angry Spacer with station personnel.

"Hey! Lucas, turn that up, please," someone sitting at a table near the bar shouted.

Naomi and Jax looked up at the same time as Lucas increased the volume. Above the bar, a row of displays was showing a mix of news, cooking shows...and one seemed to be a live camera feed of a kitten. The screen running Imperial News One caught both their eyes.

He turned. "Is that—?"

She didn't take her eyes off the screen, nodding once. "Yeah."

"Shit."

"Yeah."

Lucas came back to stand near Jax and Naomi, grabbing the tablet that controlled the screens and putting Imperial News One on all of them.

"—Station is now under control. Several senior members of Jericho station's management have been taken into custody, accused of collaborating with the Resistance. In addition, several Jericho-based enterprises have been nationalized, effective immediately," the newscaster, a blonde woman, said. She consulted the tablet before her on the desk. Smiling, she added, "We're told that damage to the station and loss of life were kept to a minimum by our brave Imperial Navy." She turned to another camera. "The Emperor has mandated a review of all independent station charters."

Like a light switch had flipped, she smiled and said, "We'll be back with more right after this."

An ad for beer replaced the news program. Lucas tapped the tablet again, muting the screens. "Holy shit."

Naomi turned to Jax. "Well, that's a bunch of shit."

The person who had asked for the volume to be increased swore. "My cousins are on Jericho." She stood and stormed out of the Angry Spacer.

Jax took a long sip of his beer, finishing it. "Lucas. Changed my mind. I'll have another." He slid the empty pint glass toward the bartender.

Naomi put a hand on his shoulder, turning him on the barstool. "Have you heard from Kori lately?"

He shook his head. "Lucas. A shot too. I don't really care what."

She nodded. "Shit."

Lucas dropped off a fresh pint and an accompanying shot of something bright green. "Think Kori's okay?"

Jax shrugged. "She's a tough one." He slammed the shot back. Making a face, he said, "Apple pucker?"

The other man grinned, nodding along with Naomi.

Naomi produced her gPhone, tapping on icons as she scowled at the device. "Jericho isn't on the Internex...like, at all."

"Not good," Lucas whispered.

Jax's gPhone beeped. After looking at the message on the screen, he picked up his new pint glass and drained it in one go. Slamming the empty glass on the counter, he turned to Naomi. "Back to work."

She frowned. "Are you sure?"

He shrugged, holding up his gPhone. "Robert is summoning us."

Naomi shook her head. "Robert."

After their adventure on Bustamonte, Jax and Naomi agreed lying low might not be a bad idea. As far as they could tell, at no point did the *Osprey*'s real ident get logged by any of the BioTek ships. However, Valerian Co-Op Infiltrators weren't abundantly common as personal spacecraft, so the odds of being connected to that job were not as close to zero as either of them would have liked.

In addition to not wanting to run into Imperial authorities that were still on the lookout for the "mystery ship" that contributed to the chaos and death toll, they also hoped to stay out of BioTek's crosshairs, if at all possible.

That meant they couldn't take jobs that required leaving Kelso station—which, both agreed, sucked.

"What took you two so long?" Robert Gunnison demanded. Arms crossed and scowling, he was waiting for them when they reached the Level 21 engineering access bay. His station employee jumpsuit was starched to the point Jax thought it could stand on its own.

"Lunch, Robert. That's what kept us," Jax replied flatly. "I'm pretty sure there's a labor code or something that guarantees a lunch break." Under his breath, he added, "Probably."

"What's so urgent?" Naomi asked.

The other man stepped to the side of the hatch he was standing in front of. "All of the fuses in Relay Junctions 21 Charlie through Foxtrot are blown." He handed Naomi one of the ruggedized tablets that everyone in station engineering used. "Map and checklist."

She took the device and checked it. "That's nearly two hundred fuses..." She looked at Robert, who smiled and held up a backpack that was near to overflowing with new fuses.

Jax snatched the bag with a grunt and headed into the engineering space without a word.

"I'll be monitoring from operations," Robert said over his shoulder as he exited the engineering space.

"Goodie," Jax drawled as the hatch closed behind the annoying station engineer.

Each level of the station had an engineering bay like this one. They provided access to sensitive equipment and components, via uncomfortable crawl spaces that ran throughout each deck like spiderwebs.

After crawling for what felt like an hour, they reached the first fuse junction. The tablet in Naomi's hand beeped. She pushed Jax's behind to make room. "Yes, Robert?"

"Are you there yet?" His voice was more nasally than normal, coming through the small device's speaker.

"We are," Jax shouted. He shoved the backpack to the side and angled himself into a semi-seated position.

Naomi turned the tablet screen around to reveal Robert staring at Jax. "Get started. I'll monitor."

Jax growled and slid open a panel in front of him to reveal row after row of scorched fuses. "What the hell happened down here anyway?"

"That asteroid cloud that passed through the area last month."

"Yeah." Jax pulled fuse after fuse, slotting a fresh one from the backpack in as he went. Each fuse was as long as his hand, about two centimeters wide, made of clear crystalline material. He fished into the bag for another clean fuse.

"The section you're in is the main power bus for the station's shields. Several power relays as well as emitters overloaded and failed during the storm. Stressed past their rating."

Naomi turned the tablet to face her. "We're not going out on the hull."

The man on the screen scoffed. "Of course not. You'd probably float off into the void and I'd get written up for losing the governor's nephew. Jackson's droid is doing the emitter repairs."

"Rudy?" Jax turned to look at Naomi and the tablet, his hand drifting toward the useless socket. A spark leaped from the contact to his knuckle. He swore and snatched his hand back, almost smacking himself in the face.

"Careful, you dummy," Robert scolded.

"Pretty sure he meant Baxter," Naomi offered.

Jax slotted the fuse.

On the tablet, Robert nodded. "Okay, those all look good. Head for Delta junction."

"You did something wrong. That last one isn't registering," Robert scolded from the tablet screen.

Jax eyed the last fuse he slotted. He clucked, removed it, wiped both ends on his shirt, and slotted it again. "Better?"

Robert nodded.

"Only twelve more," Naomi offered. She was now in charge of pulling fresh fuses from one section of the bag and depositing the burned-out units in the other side of the bag. She offered Jax a fuse.

He extended his hand, but stopped short when his gPhone rang. His eyes went wide.

Naomi's eyes also went wide. "Isn't that the ringtone for—"

Jax nodded. He fished the ringing device out of a thigh pocket and looked at the screen. He held the device so Naomi could see the screen as well, then accepted the call.

"Excuse me. You're on the—" Robert started to say, but the rest was muffled when Naomi sat the tablet face down on the crawl space floor and pushed it away from her with her foot. Robert's muffled, indignant shouts continued.

"Jax? You there?" Kori's voice asked.

"Yeah, Kori. I'm here. Naomi is too. You okay? Where are you?"

On the small screen, Kori's face visibly relaxed. "I'm here. And, yeah, I'm okay. Got off Jericho just in time." She looked ragged, adding, "Barely."

"Here where?" Naomi asked.

Jax nodded his agreement with the question.

"Kelso. Or, well, I will be in a minute. On approach. Docking shortly."

"We'll meet you in the bay," Jax said before he started to squirm his way around in the tight crawl space. He stopped. "Which bay?"

"Four," Kori answered.

He smiled. "See you soon." He ended the call and stuffed the device into his pocket. He resumed his squirming, trying to make his way around Naomi.

She shoved him. "Stop pushing. I'll go first!"

A muffled series of expletives came from the tablet a meter away.

Jax grabbed the backpack, fishing out fuses while Naomi crawled backwards to the tablet.

"—take this job seriously," Robert was shouting. He realized he wasn't looking at the deck plating and composed himself. "You two are the most unprof—"

"Robert." Naomi cut him off. "Get on with it." She looked at Jax, who was pulling and replacing fuses as quickly as he could without getting shocked. Except he got shocked every fourth or fifth fuse and was swearing louder and louder with each shock.

Robert grumbled but said nothing, looking at something off screen. "Those check out," he said, a moment later adding, "Those too. Okay, all fuses—"

"Great, thanks, Robert!" Naomi said around a wide, super fake smile. She tapped the icon to disconnect the call. As she shoved the tablet into the backpack with the burned-out fuses, she said, "Let's go."

Jax nodded his agreement.

As much as they wanted to hurry, there was simply no way to crawl back to the engineering junction faster than they were going. The touch deck plating in the crawl space was painful at a slow pace and nearly crippling when rushing.

"I hate these spaces," Jax huffed as they reached the end, standing slowly to stretch his back. "Stupid gig work."

Naomi nodded her agreement, tossing the backpack to the ground with a crystalline clink. "Robert can get these here. Let's go."

The main docking structure was several levels below them. As it was nearing the end of what most folks called Alpha Shift, the corridors were getting crowded and the lift cars were doing their best to move people up and down the length of the station as quickly and efficiently as possible.

Jax tapped Naomi's elbow, nodding toward a service hatch off to the side of the central bank of lifts. She followed him. Several people watched the pair as they stepped out of the crowd waiting for a lift car.

He waved his gPhone across the small panel next to the hatch. With a soft beep, the hatch slid open. Turning to Naomi, he winked.

The space to the side of the public lifts, protected by a secure hatch, held two service lifts. They were larger than their people-moving cousins and nothing but bare metal walls and a control panel. The wait for a service lift was far shorter than the wait out in the public lift lobby. They were moving down to the docks in short order.

The docking bay was as busy as ever. The main lift lobby was a massive multistory affair with windows looking into the lobby above four heavy bulkhead doors, all open unless one of the four docking bays became compromised.

Naomi looked at the four huge pressure doors. "Which bay?"

Jax made a face. He pulled out his gPhone. When the call connected, he asked, "What bay? Oh, okay. See ya soon." He turned to Naomi. "Four." He pointed to the door behind her, a meter-tall 4 painted on the bulkhead over it.

Bay 4 was a hive of activity. A few dozen ships of various sizes were coming and going. The pair looked around. Spotting the ship they thought was Kori's, they headed toward the landing grid it was aiming for.

"Hey! Hey, you two!"

Jax turned to see Kori walking down the steps of a small blue and gray shuttle. She waved. "Guess that's her ship." They jogged over to the sleek craft, pulling their friend into a group hug.

"So glad you're safe," Jax whispered into Kori's hair.

Naomi held the other woman at arm's length. "Tell us

everything." She turned and led the group back toward the bay's exit.

Kori took a deep breath. "I don't think I've ever been that scared. They showed up and surrounded the station. Before I'd made it halfway to the office, they were firing on us."

"They attacked the station?" Jax asked. He knew the news was slanting the story toward the Imperial side of things, but hiding the fact that they shot first? He nodded to himself. Easy to believe.

Kori nodded. Goose bumps flashed across her arms as she remembered the chaos. "Yeah. Then the station returned fire, and that's when it got crazy. I think the station took out one of the Imperial ships, a small one. I saw debris before I got clear." She shook her head. "Or they were shooting the ships that fled."

They reached the lift lobby and waited for the next lift. Once underway, Kori continued. "I got out just before they interdicted the entire area."

"Damn," Jax hissed. "Interdiction?"

Kori ran a hand over the top of her mid length Afro, patting it back into shape. "Three heavies, a couple of corvettes, and the interdictor." She looked at each of her friends in turn. "What're they saying?"

Naomi shook her head. "That Jericho was a base of operations for the Resistance and attacked the navy first."

The other woman shook her head. "Bullshit. Guessing they didn't mention any casualties?" Jax and Naomi shook their heads. "Fuckers," she hissed.

The lift doors slid apart on Deck 34, where Jax and Naomi both had quarters. He looked at his ex-girlfriend. "My bed is your bed."

"Your bed is my bed, and your bed is the couch," she replied without missing a beat.

He coughed. "Wait. No—that's not what I meant." He stopped. "Unless?"

"No."

He held up both hands. "Okay. Okay." Under his breath, he added, "Your loss."

She looked at him. "No, it ain't."

CHAPTER 2

"It's not that bad," Jax said. Again.

Baxter, standing near the *Osprey* in the Caruso family mechanical bay, turned to Jax. "It is beneath me."

Jax shrugged. "What isn't? You're a combat bot." He gestured at the droid's feet. "At least you don't need an EVA suit and clunky mag boots." He smiled. "You are a clunky mag boot."

The matte black droid took a step forward. "I will clunky mag boot you."

Kori and Naomi were at a card table that served as the mech bay's dining table. This morning, the former's hair was in two uniform puffs, one on either side of her head. "So, you two are just doing—"

"Three," Baxter cut in.

Kori smiled. "You three are doing grunt work around the station?"

Naomi nodded, holding up a finger to silence Jax. "Yeah, we're lying low. After the whole thing with BioTek, we thought we'd keep a low profile for a bit. Let folks forget that a Valerian Infiltrator was in all the news broadcasts for almost an entire month."

The other woman chuckled. "Yeah, you two are fantastic at calling attention to yourselves. Surprised your friends on the *Resolute* or *Justicar* didn't put the pieces together."

Jax cleared his throat. "Yeah, lucky."

Rudy rolled over, tablet clutched in one little metal hand. "Robert's on the tablet." He thrust the device toward Jax, who held both hands up and took a step back.

Naomi sighed and motioned that she'd take the device. "Hi, Robert."

"Where are you two?" the face on the screen demanded.

She rolled her eyes. "We'll be there in a few."

"The docking bay service level isn't rewiring itself."

"If it could, he'd just turn it off and make us do it," Jax said.

"I heard that."

"Darn."

Naomi waved Jax away. "We've got a friend in town. She'll come help."

Kori leaned back. "I will?"

"Just hurry up," the face on the screen demanded before disconnecting.

"He's pleasant," Kori said.

"He grows on ya," Jax said.

Naomi made a face. "Robert, the senior engineering department lead. He's who we've been working for."

Jax nodded to Kori. "We better get you some clothes you don't mind lighting on fire later." At her confused look, he said, "The docking bay service level is the sub-floor under the bay. Where all the umbilicals and shit are."

"Emphasis on the shit," Rudy offered on his way up the *Osprey*'s boarding ramp. As he rolled, he said, "Have fun."

Baxter, his ruby red optic sensor swishing back and forth, said, "If you need me, I'll be on the hull of the station."

The docking bay service level was exactly as disgusting as Jax warned the two women. Robert assigned them Bay 1 and the repair and replacement of umbilicals from power to bilge.

"You know, when I fled potentially being killed by the Empire, I didn't think the reward would be cleaning out literal shit from under spaceships," Kori said. Grease had flattened one of her perfectly spherical hair puffs.

The trio was sitting under the engine nacelle of a midsized Ny Sverige-flagged freighter eating sandwiches Rudy had dropped off earlier.

Jax nodded. "I'm sure Robert will have notes." He grunted. "Hate that guy."

Naomi's gPhone sang a sad little song, drawing Jax and Kori's gaze. She frowned and pulled the phone out of a pocket on her vest. After looking at her two friends, she focused on the phone, a new message from an account she never expected to see a message from.

Her mom.

Naomi watched the video while Kori and Jax shared a few awkward glances. When she finished, she didn't move.

"Naomi?" Jax said. "You okay?" She blinked, then handed the phone to him. He looked at the screen, then leaned closer to Kori so she could watch with him. He hit play.

An elderly Asian woman's face appeared. "Hello, Omi." Jax glanced up at Naomi, eyebrow raised. She gave him a tight nod. The woman on the screen continued. "We need your help. We're on Shise, and the Imperials just arrived. They're talking about blockading the colony." The woman looked off screen. Some type of commotion was happening nearby. She turned back to the camera. "People are panicking here, including us. Please, Omi." The recording stopped.

Jax looked at his friend and business partner, handing the gPhone back. "Damn."

Naomi nodded.

Kori cocked her head to one side. "I thought you didn't talk to your folks."

"I don't," Naomi confirmed. "Not since..." She ran a hand over her hair, fidgeting with her ponytail. "I didn't even know they'd moved to Shise."

Kori scooted closer to Naomi, putting an arm around the other woman's slender shoulders.

Jax slid the remains of his lunch away and pulled his own gPhone out of a pocket. "Skip, get ready to fly."

"Copy that, Captain," the *Osprey*'s managing Sapient Intelligence replied.

Naomi looked at him. "It's too risky."

"You're the one that's been teaching me to let people in and all. They're your family."

Kori's eyes went wide. She turned to Naomi. "You fixed him?"

The other woman shook her head. "I wouldn't go that far."

"I'm literally right here," Jax said. He tapped another icon on his phone. "Bax, get back in. We're leaving soon."

"Thank whatever mechanical god looks over droids," the big combat bot replied.

Naomi smiled. While she wasn't sure fixing Jackson Caruso was possible, he was beginning to feel like what she imagined a brother felt like. She'd grown up wanting a brother, but her parents had always been too focused on their careers.

You're lucky we had you. They would joke whenever she asked about siblings. She thought after being shipped off, watching kids in the program vanish, and living on the run, that she'd be over siblings. Meeting Jax on Mariposa sparked that old feeling again.

It'd take some more work, but maybe he'd make an okay almost-brother. Eventually. She blinked the random thoughts away. "You can stay in my quarters if you like."

Kori affected a stricken look. "There's no scenario where I don't go with you two."

Naomi smiled. "Thanks."

"I'm gonna go talk to Auntie, let her know we're taking off for a bit."

"Better shower first," Kori said.

Jax raised an arm to sniff his sleeve and nodded. "Good call."

The trip from his quarters to the administrative levels of Kelso station didn't take long. The lunch rush was winding down. Most station personnel were wherever they needed to be for the rest of what passed for "daytime" on the station.

When he entered the lobby of the station governor's office, he waved to Jeffry. "She busy?"

Before the other man could answer, the sound of shouting came from behind the closed doors to the governor's office.

Jax made a face and dropped into a seat near Jeffry's desk. "Glad I'm not in there."

The younger man nodded. "It's been like that since yesterday."

"Jericho?"

"Yup."

The doors opened and several people Jax knew only by reputation stalked out, some looking angrier than others. None looked happy. Department heads and members of founding families, the latter feeling their opinions counted for at least twice what everyone else's did, were all demanding the governor "do something."

After the crowd passed, he spotted his adoptive aunt, Governor Neeti Singh. She spotted Jax and smiled. "Hello, Jackson. What fresh hell have you brought to my doorstep today?" Jax faked a pained expression. "Don't make that face. You and trouble go hand in hand."

Jax wobbled his head, a gesture he had picked up from the governor when he was a child. "Okay, that's fair. Promise, though. No trouble." He followed her into the office, taking a seat opposite her desk. "What was that all about?"

She made waved a dismissive hand in the air. "Nervous nellies. This Jericho business has the lot of them freaking out."

"I kinda thought station founders were made of sterner stuff."

The governor smoothed her mostly jet-black hair. "Bah. Children and grandchildren of founding families. Living off their forbearers' hard work." While some members of founding families held high-level jobs, others lived off the taxes the station collected and by charter split among the founders. Governor Singh held a dim view of the latter.

She shook her head. "Anyway. What did you come up here for? Surely not to listen to me gripe about skittish socialites."

He chuckled. "Fun as that sounds, no. I just wanted to let you know we're taking off. Naomi's parents need help."

Governor Singh leaned back in her chair. "I didn't think they spoke."

Jax gave a shrug. "Recent development. They're on Shise, and the Empire's up to something."

"When aren't they?" She locked her gaze on his. "You'll be careful? No shenanigans. No picking fights with mega corps."

Jax grinned. "Scout's honor."

"You were never a scout."

"Then your mileage may vary." He stood. "We shouldn't be long. Just gonna pick 'em up and come back here to get things sorted."

The governor nodded. "Please be careful. I don't know what's going on out there. The Imperials are suddenly taking the Resistance seriously."

Jax nodded, but kept his mouth shut. He and Naomi had told no one that they were working with the Resistance. Not the Delphinos, not Kori, and most certainly not his aunt.

He smiled. "Will do. Good luck keeping folks calm here."

She returned the smile. "I'll need it."

While Jax was cleaning up and talking to the governor, Naomi and Kori worked with Rudy to get the *Osprey* ready for travel.

Kori exited the ship's head, toweling off her hair. She was in a borrowed pale purple jumpsuit that Naomi had long ago found in the closet of her berth and held onto.

"Thanks for doing this," she said after joining Naomi in her berth. They'd agreed to share Naomi's room so that the elder Himuras could have a berth to themselves once they picked them up.

"I've slept on the couch out there. It'd be a war crime to make you sleep on that."

Kori laughed. "I meant...well, yeah, that couch sucks, but I meant letting me crash with you. You know, after—"

Naomi waved a hand. "Don't mention it."

"I'm glad you guys were here." She lowered her voice. "Don't tell Jax. I called Marshall first."

Naomi laughed. "I'll hold on to it for the next time he annoys me."

"So, next week then."

The two women laughed until Rudy came in. "What's so funny?"

"Nothing." Naomi waved a hand. "Jax back?"

The little rust-colored droid bobbed up and down on his smart material roller ball, the closest he could get to a nod. "We should be ready to depart in ten." He turned and rolled back toward the front of the ship.

Naomi stood. "Might as well go watch our departure, then we can make up the other berth. It hasn't been used for a few months." She made a face. "Not sure what state it's in."

The pair made their way from the crew berths at the aft of the *Osprey*'s common deck.

Naomi had only been working with Jax for a little over two years, but after the BioTek thing and their decision to lie low, this was the longest she'd not been aboard the *Osprey*. It shocked her how weird it felt and, at the same time, how comfortable it was coming back.

Walking into the lounge space, Kori smiled. "Good to see this place is still a hot mess."

Naomi quirked an eyebrow. "And this is cleaned up." She made air quotes as she said it.

Kori made a disgusted face. "I don't know how you do it." They headed for the spiral staircase that traversed the three decks of the ship.

Naomi grunted. "I meditate a lot."

The other woman laughed.

Jax looked over his shoulder as the two women arrived on the small flight deck. Naomi moved to her station while Kori found a spot to lean on a console near the back. "Hi, ladies. All set?" Both nodded. He turned forward and said, "Skip, status?"

"Baxter is in the hold, reporting ready. Station space control has cleared us."

Jax nodded and began flipping the switches that controlled the mechanical bay's systems remotely. A pale blue outline snapped to life around the inner edge of the large exterior doors as orange strobes came to life. A moment later, those doors slid apart. Orange strobes in the bay's ceiling kicked on, warning anyone in the bay that the outer doors were open.

The *Osprey* rose off of her birdlike landing gear. As the

ship's weight moved off them, the gear stretched, then retracted, folding up into compartments in either wing root.

An indicator on Jax's console flipped from red to green when the mechanical bay's outer doors were fully open. He eased the throttle forward. "Here we go. Fingers crossed there's not a BioTek ship waiting for us."

"Not funny," Naomi said.

The *Osprey* slid out of the mechanical bay and joined the outbound traffic, making its way clear of the station. The station mandated a one-thousand-kilometer buffer where ripping open space-time was strictly prohibited.

Ahead of them, a personal yacht opened a wormhole and vanished.

"We're up next," Jax announced. He leaned forward and powered up the *Osprey*'s wormhole generator. As the ship passed the entry/exit threshold, he activated the generator. A swirling orange and purple rupture opened ahead of them. Within seconds, the ship had passed into the tunnel through normal time and space, the opening, closing behind them.

CHAPTER 3

"How is it you have pizza?" Kori asked, setting her slice back on the plate.

Jax winked. "Forethought."

From the little charging base near the bulkhead-mounted display, Rudy's optic sensor lit up. "Come again?"

Jax rolled his eyes. "By forethought, I meant Rudy thought of the pizza."

"Thank you," the droid said before his optic sensor dimmed.

Kori watched all this, then took another bite. "Well, it's good." She looked at the wall display. "Mario Kart?"

Naomi tossed her slice onto the box top. "I call Luigi!"

While Jax sifted through the entertainment menus looking for the hundreds of years old game, he said, "So, life on Jericho. Good?"

Kori gave him a hand wobble. "Good enough. My boss is a good guy. His business has been growing. There's five of us on staff now."

Naomi watched as the game entered "pick your driver"

mode. She began moving through the options. "Promotion? You didn't mention that."

Kori reached up to her Afro, patting it. She'd teased out her customary matching smaller Afro puffs when she came aboard, opting for one large puff. She smiled. "Well. Yeah." She grinned. "He added two new offices in the next sector. I'm heading up security for all of them."

Naomi nodded. "Way to go!" She offered a hand for her friend to high five.

Jax finished customizing his cartoon racer. "You two ready?"

"You picked the monkey?" Kori asked, finalizing the color pallet of her character's motorcycle.

"I'm seeing if I can beat the game with each character." He held up a finger. "I did Mario," another finger, "Princess Peach," another finger, "and Toad." He smiled. "Now Donkey Kong."

He gestured to the screen. "Let's go."

The group was gathered on the bridge. The swirl of space-time outside the bridge windows shifted then vanished as the *Osprey* slipped back into normal space.

The ruddy sphere of Shise was directly ahead, growing in size. Nearly a dozen Imperial corvettes and a light cruiser were spread out in orbit, along with a smattering of mid-size and bulk freighters. It didn't look like the Empire had sent any of its bigger capital ships.

"Welcome to Shise," Jax drawled. "The party has definitely already started." One corvette was docked alongside a freighter, likely inspecting it.

Naomi looked at her sensor display. "At least none of the big ones are here." She went back to checking over the sensor readings.

"Take the wins we can get," Jax said under his breath. Not that a bunch of corvettes and a light cruiser were anything to take lightly, but they weren't a capital ship, so there was that.

Kori leaned over Jax's shoulder. "Oh man. I hate mole towns."

"Come again?" Naomi said. She looked up from her console again, first at Kori, then at Rudy, who did his best approximation of a shrug.

Kori pointed out the forward window. "Underground colonies. So...dismal."

Jax looked up at her. "Dismal? Word of the day calendar?"

She turned to him and clucked. "Boy."

He leaned away. "Anyway, yeah, underground colonies aren't my favorite either." He looked over his shoulder. "Either of you ever been here before?" Both women shook their heads.

Ahead of them the glittering lights of the capital city's domes and various sensor and communication towers were coming into view.

Jax adjusted their course. "Hopefully, with all the traffic, the Imperials aren't paying too much attention. Maybe they decided a full blockade was overkill."

"Incoming hail," Skip said.

"Or not," Jax said with a sigh. He pushed the throttle forward and sent the *Osprey* toward the planet's southern pole. "Ignore them."

"A sound strategy," the ceiling replied.

Kori shook her head. "Like old times."

As the *Osprey* accelerated, several smaller Imperial ships pulled away from their formation.

"Three corvettes are moving to intercept. They are also hailing us. Again," Skip informed. "I assume I should I continue to ignore them?"

"Yup," Jax said without taking his eyes off the heads-up display. He reached his left hand out to a section of his control console, activating the *Osprey*'s electronic counter-measure systems. If they could lose the corvettes quickly, they could find a place to land without getting caught.

Across the transparent forward window, a ghostly green arrow was pointing toward the planet's southern pole, Skip updating the heads-up display in real time as they flew. He was also adding faint red arrows to show the flight paths of the three corvettes attempting to converge on them.

Kori, still standing behind Jax's seat, asked, "So, what exactly is the plan?"

Jax nodded toward the forward window. "Looks like there's a lot of air traffic coming and going. If we can get into atmo, without being destroyed, we can blend in and find a place to land. Skip, activate those new do-dads, optical whammy array?" He glanced over his shoulder. "By the way, do we know where we're going?"

Sounding annoyed, Skip said, "Activating visual distraction system." A series of panels along the hull energized, pumping out random EM fields and the occasional holographic blob or spark. Any ship trying to get a visual fix on the small ship would see a shifting field of energy and colors flickering around the hull, making visual identification more difficult. Coupled with the ECM suite throwing out random identifier codes and electronic noise, the *Osprey* was invisible in more or less plain sight.

After their Empire-spanning adventure with the now

former VP of loss prevention and IP protection at BioTek, Jax had sprung for a few more goodies to keep them from being easily identified.

"Oh, uh..." Naomi glanced over to Rudy. "One second."

"There are three main colonial hubs on Shise: Ny Hokkaido, Morriston, and Ny Gifu," the nav droid offered.

Kori made a face. "And?" She turned to Naomi.

The other woman made a reciprocal face. "I, uh... Working on it."

"No rush," Jax said. He glanced to the right, following the three ghostly red arrows toward the three Imperial corvettes that were now much, much closer to the *Osprey*. "Skip, are they in—" The lead ship fired. A bolt of energy lanced across the *Osprey*'s bow. The lighting on the bridge flicked to red. Jax pulled the flight controls hard over to the left. "Never mind." He pushed the flight control forward, putting the *Osprey* into a dive before sending them into a spiral. The planet Shise was spinning in and out of view through the forward window.

Kori darted toward the back of the small bridge, grabbing handholds to keep from falling. "Never a dull moment."

The *Osprey* banked and swerved as it plunged toward the planet's upper atmosphere.

"All corvettes are now within weapons range," Skip announced.

The ship shook as several energy bolts slammed into the *Osprey*'s shields.

"Almost there," Jax kept repeating to himself. On the

heads-up display, the green arrow flickered out. "Hey, wait...What?"

"I did not think you required guidance to the planet, it being right in front of us and all," Skip offered.

"Here we go!" Naomi shouted. "Found 'em!" She tapped a few controls and sent the information to Rudy, who beeped his acknowledgement.

The ghostly green arrow reappeared on the heads-up display, accompanied by a series of details about their destination. "Ny Hokkaido, here we—" The *Osprey* rattled violently. Outside the window, the ship's shields flickered and pulsed a dull orange. "Hold on!" Jax shouted over the din of alarm klaxons. "Skip?" The alarms fell silent.

Their forward shields glowed as the ship began its atmospheric interface.

"The corvettes are slowing. They are not entering the atmosphere," Skip announced.

Jax adjusted their course, angling away from Ny Hokkaido Spaceport.

"Uh, where are we going?" Naomi asked.

"We'll head for the next nearest port, start blending in, then circle back. Skip, disable the visual-whatsit."

"Done," Skip confirmed.

As the visual distraction system shut down, Jax guided the *Osprey* in alongside a mid-size freighter en route to Morriston. After a few minutes, he reached forward and disabled the ECM suite, letting their forged but legit-looking transponder ident activate. As far as anyone above or below them was concerned, they were the light transport *Velma*.

"Okay, turning about. Want to call and make sure we've got a parking spot?"

"Ny Hokkaido Spaceport confirms landing clearance,"

Naomi offered. "They're not sure why or how we just appeared on their scopes, but given everything going on, were fine not asking questions. Sending our clearance and landing instructions to your console."

From the back of the bridge, Kori said, "I'm more worried about leaving." She looked at a status display over Naomi's console. "Skip, is this..."

"Bad? Yes," the ship's SI said.

"What?" Jax asked from up front. He didn't look back but did glance at his own ship's status display, noticing a blinking red icon. They were on approach to the spaceport, a series of bright lights guiding them in over the blustery orange and brown landscape of Shise. Massive fungi ridges as big as skyscrapers dotted the landscape, making the final approach interesting.

"Those large fungi are one of Shise's chief exports," Skip offered.

"No one asked," Jax replied.

"It apparently tastes much like beef when seasoned properly. It is also—"

"Dude!" Jax shouted.

"Anyway. That last strike by the Imperials—" Skip said. One of the forward displays came to life, showing a diagram of the ship. "—Damaged the energy dampener matrix. It will need to be repaired, or better yet, replaced. You will need to find a binary phase coil while we are here."

"We can't limp along without?" Jax asked. Limping along without things was common practice for him. Things that could be ignored were.

"Negative. Without the dampener matrix, any stray exotic energy flux could overload our systems. Best case, we would end up stranded in deep space. Worst, we would be destroyed."

The *Osprey* flew over a small rise, the opening to the spaceport now visible as a thick duracrete dome with a large static atmosphere-barrier-protected opening in the dome's top came into view. The ship rattled as Jax eased back the throttle.

Ny Hokkaido's spaceport complex was a dome a kilometer in diameter. The opening at the very top was large enough for ships three times the size of the *Osprey* to descend through. The interior was ringed by three large balconies filled with ships of all sizes and shapes. The ground level had several huge repair bays arrayed around the perimeter on either side of the main entrance.

Jax lowered the *Osprey* to the beta level landing ring, slowly rotating the ship until he saw the large 5 painted on the dome's inner wall. Pushing the throttle one notch forward, he eased the ship over their designated parking place.

Naomi leaned to look out the window on her side of the bridge. "Looks like folks aren't planning on sticking around long." There was a line of people snaking from the entry of the spaceport to a large idling personnel transport.

"Probably not a bad idea," Kori said, adding, "all things considered."

As the *Osprey* slid toward her appointed parking place on her lift engines, people looked up from their tasks. Luggage and small cargo modules were stacked near almost every ship on beta level.

Jax spun the *Osprey* around, then eased her back into the assigned space. A pair of metallic clanks announced the bird-leg-like landing gear were deploying. Several additional clanks and clunks announced that the gear were fully deployed and locked into position. With a reduction in power to the lift engines, the ship sank onto her landing gear with a groan.

Jax flipped a few overhead switches, causing the low rumble of the ship's reactor to fade.

"Reactor is now at standby power," Skip announced.

Jax stood. "Rudy, get a list of parts we'll need to make repairs to the...whatsit?"

"Energy dampener matrix," Skip offered.

The small navigation droid released the clips that held him at his console. "Copy that."

Jax gestured to the stairs. "Let's go find some old people."

Baxter met them in the cargo hold. Jax shook his head. "Afraid you two need to stay behind. This place isn't so fringe that droids move around freely. We wouldn't make it twenty feet before someone freaked out. And with everything going on upstairs..." He shook his head.

"I never get to have any fun," Baxter complained. He had his cloak in one hand.

Kori spotted the garment. "Is that a cloak?" She turned to Jax.

"Don't ask." He shook his head and turned to Naomi. "We'll meet you at your parents' place?"

Naomi nodded. "Sounds good. I'll message their address once I find them."

"How will you find them?" Rudy asked.

Naomi made a face. "I'm hoping there's a directory somewhere."

"You can't call them?" Kori asked.

Naomi shook her head. "They used a one-time account when they called me." She shrugged.

The boarding ramp lowered, unfolding as it did. The

group filed down a separate set of stairs into the small boarding room at the lowest deck of the ship. It wasn't very large, with room enough for only two or three people. They filed out onto the duracrete of the spaceport.

CHAPTER 4

"Well, here we are again," Rudy said as he dropped through the center of the spiral staircase. The special null gravity channel that ran through all three decks allowed him to quickly move about the ship.

Baxter, standing perfectly still, said, "The joys of being a droid. I like it better when we stick to fringe colonies."

"Like you two have anything to complain about," Skip said from the overhead speakers. "You get to leave the ship. Go out into the stations and colonies. I'm stuck sitting in spaceports. You know who I get to talk to? Moronic RIs that only want to talk about navigation and resource management."

Most ships after the war pulled their Sapient Intelligences, replacing them with more simplistic Rudimentary Intelligences that were restricted to navigation and basic ship's functions.

"Titillating," Baxter said.

"Still probably less annoying that dealing with humans," Rudy offered.

The trio shared what passed for laughter among droids.

Switching to the shared wireless network, Skip sent, *We may have a problem.*

BAXTER: *What is it?*

SKIP: *Sending data.*

RUDY: *Oh hell. Is that—*

SKIP: *Imperial patrol? Yes.*

BAXTER: *We can take them.*

Rudy turned to his much larger friend and shook his flat, cylindrical head. He rolled toward the hatch set in the forward bulkhead. Opening it, he rolled into the workshop and sort-of armory. Reaching the next forward bulkhead, he waited.

Skip triggered a thick, well-hidden hatch to unlock and swing into the room.

Rudy's head spun to look back the way he came. *Come on.*

Baxter sent a frowning emoji wirelessly, then followed the small navigation droid into the only smuggling compartment on the ship that could hold the massive droid.

Outside the ship, a young-looking naval officer and two shock troops approached the *Osprey*.

"Is this the ship, sir?" one of the troopers asked in their heavily modulated voice, his matte gray armor reflecting none of the harsh overhead lighting.

The young lieutenant smoothed his crimson uniform before checking the military grade tablet in his hand. "It is a Valerian Co-Op Infiltrator like the one seen breaking through the blockade, but the name and registry don't match."

"How many ships like this could there be?" the other trooper asked. "It's a relic."

The lieutenant made a face and looked over the two trooper's shoulders to point. Up on the second level, another infiltrator sat. It was dark blue like the *Osprey,* but someone had added stark white racing stripes to the wings.

He turned back to the *Osprey.* "Let's take a look inside." He held his tablet up and sent the Imperial override that all ships were required to have and that Jax never bothered to install when his arrived on Kelso station twenty-odd years ago.

Skip sighed as he saw through a camera what the Imperial was doing. When his transceiver received the code, he thought about ignoring it. He knew that if he did, the Imperials would get suspicious and call in a ship breaking team to force their way in.

With a hiss, the *Osprey*'s boarding ramp lowered, half of it unfolding as it did.

While the nosy Imperials crept up the ramp, he spun up the false RI that would act as a shield while he interacted with the intruders. He also hacked into the spaceport's management array, tweaking their entry data just enough to throw the Imperials off the scent.

Pointing to one of the troopers, the lieutenant said, "Go up and check the common deck and bridge." He gestured to the other. "Follow me." He headed aft toward the engineering spaces.

In the forward smuggling compartment, Rudy and Baxter waited. As a safety precaution, both had powered down as much as possible should the Imperials have more powerful sensors.

Skip watched the first trooper check the head and the crew berths before making their way to the stairs and the bridge. The lieutenant and second trooper reached engineering, the former plugging his tablet into the diagnostic interface.

So insulting and intrusive, Skip thought as he fended off each probe from the tablet, shunting the search threads to fake results in a specially fire walled partition in his computer core.

"So do you even know what a binary phase coil looks like?" Kori asked as she and Jax entered the nearest commercial district from the spaceport.

He shrugged. "Nope." He held up his gPhone so she could see the screen. "Rudy sent me a few pictures." He swiped through a few pics of a ship part he'd never understand the function of, then blushed and lowered his phone.

"Saw that," Kori said.

"Sorry."

"Still enjoying what the field has to offer, I see." She gave him a knowing smirk. "He seems to have plenty to offer." Seeing Jax blush brought a smile to her face. She nodded down a narrow side corridor. The commercial zone was made up of numerous criss-crossing tunnels several meters wide, with stalls and shops carved into the walls. The smaller side corridors that occasionally branched off so far seemed to have shops only on one side and were half as wide as the main tunnels.

"I'll settle down when I meet the right person. Probably." Jax followed her into the tunnel. The wayfinding signage overhead indicated that this tunnel was starship parts and salvagers.

Kori grinned. "Not sure what's scarier: you settling down or the idea of the person who could lead to you settling down."

"I feel attacked," he replied with a grin. "That looks promising." At the end of the tunnel, a flickering neon sign read Melvin's Vintage Parts and Scrap. "We'll not mention to Skip where the parts came from."

Kori nodded her agreement.

The door to the Melvin's Vintage Parts and Scrap was unlocked. The interior of the shop was far larger than the door had implied. Either Melvin had paid for more space or, and more likely, he'd been illegally adding to his space. The claw marks on some of the walls gave Jax the answer. He shook his head.

From a counter near the back, a voice said, "Come on in! Let me know if you need help."

The pair made their way toward the counter, Jax saying, "Actually, yeah. We're looking for a binary..." He scratched his head.

"Binary phase coil," Kori offered.

"Yeah, that," Jax said.

"For an energy dampener matrix," Kori added.

A small woman with skin darker than Kori's popped into view. "For what type of ship?"

Jax consulted his gPhone. He recalled Rudy including a note with the pictures. There it was. "A class four alpha. Valerian Co-Op Infiltrator, to be exact."

"Interesting!" she replied. "Follow me." She came out from behind the counter and headed off between two massive shelves. Over her shoulder, she said, "Don't see many folks shopping for parts for older Valerian jobs much anymore."

"Family heirloom," Jax said.

"So, what happens if people need bigger parts?" Kori asked, running her hand along the shelf as she walked, noting the various bins, none larger than a foot or two wide.

"Like what? Engines?" The shopkeeper, obviously not Melvin, asked.

"Sure, like engines," Jax said.

"They go somewhere else," she answered. After making a turn, she took them deeper into the shop to a section excavated more recently, if the floor and walls were an indication. "Here we are." She pulled a large bin partially off the shelf. "Goddamnit," she hissed.

"Problem?" Jax asked. He moved his hand toward the shelf next to him, gripping the bin there.

The little scrap seller held up a wrinkly piece of paper she'd found in the bin she was holding. "My no-good ex took all the binary phase coils." The note read, "Booboo, borrowed your phase coils. Happy to trade for you know what. XOXO, Big Fudge."

Kori sighed. "Okay, well, I guess we'll be going." She turned, putting a hand on Jax's shoulder.

The other woman crumpled the note, tossing it in the empty bin. "Hold on a minute."

Jax turned to look at the small woman. "Look, we don't have time. If you don't have the part we need..." He shrugged. "No offense."

"You won't find any coils elsewhere. Why do you think my idiot ex took mine? They're not exactly common pieces of tech these days. Newer ships use a different technology." Jax groaned. "Look kids. I had four binary phase coils. You need one. Go...liberate them, and the one you need is on the house."

"Why'd your ex steal them?" Kori demanded. "Specifically?"

"And what's he want in trade?" Jax added.

The older woman shrugged. "Binary phase coils are one of those pieces of tech that are more or less forgettable... until yours breaks." She grinned. "That's why I have them all. They don't take up much space and when someone shows up needing one," she rubbed her hands together, "I get to set the price." She grimaced. "As to what that wrinkled old shyster wants in trade...Well, he ain't gettin' it."

Jax and Kori exchanged a look. The former finally sighed. "Fine. Where can we find, I presume, Melvin aka Big Fudge?"

"And how do we get in?" the latter asked.

The older woman smiled, her teeth gleaming in stark contrast to her skin.

The three major cities of Shise were nearly identical in their layout; each city was arrayed in concentric circles around the massive city center dome. The spaceports, much larger domes, were set off to the side of each city, distant enough that any catastrophe wouldn't impact the city itself. All connected by maglev trains.

The walk from the train station to the tunnel opening of the first section of the residential ring didn't take Naomi long. It did give her time to think about what she'd say to her parents. Thankfully, each major intersection had a colony directory. Each tunnel had a torii gate at its entrance.

Despite the Imperial ships overhead, it was not as chaotic on the ground as she worried it would be. It sounded far more chaotic in her mother's video message. She shook her head. People seemed to be going about their business as usual, oblivious to the Imperial presence in orbit. Here and there she spotted a sign of unease, but otherwise, the Imperial ships seemed to be as much a curiosity as a concern. She was starting to think that those folks lining up for that personnel hauler were just everyday traffic.

After living on Kelso station for the last two years and moving around as much as she had prior to that, being surrounded by mostly Japanese people was a bit jarring. She thought about the various worlds in the Nippon sector and how the Japanese, upon fleeing Earth, had stuck together more than so many other nationalities.

The Itabashi neighborhood was quite nice. Immaculately polished white acrylic panels lined the tunnel walls. The floors were a dull gray permacrete with delicate filagree patterns and kanji to mark intersections and even residential addresses.

The door to each residential unit was decorated and had a family name in neat calligraphy over it.

She took a deep a breath. "Here we go." She pressed the announcer button.

A minute later, the door slid open to reveal an older woman, her hair in a neat bun at the back of her head. She was in a simple but well-maintained outfit of canvas pants and shirt. Her mother.

The older woman blinked several times. "Omi?"

Naomi raised a hand. "Hi, Mom."

The other woman moved faster than Naomi would have thought possible, lunging to wrap her in a hug that threatened to collapse a lung. "Mom...Mom, I can't breathe."

"Oh, sorry, dear." Her mother released her. "I can't believe you came."

From inside, her father shouted, "Daarin! Who is it?"

Naomi's mother turned. "Hanii, Omi is here!" Her

father made an excited noise. Her mother ushered her inside.

Her father was standing in the living room. "You came." He clasped his hands in front of him, offering a slight bow.

"You called." Naomi approached him.

The Himura residence was a simple affair. The entry led into an open plan living room and kitchen space. Off to the side was a hallway that led to the single bedroom. Opposite that was a door to the washroom.

Several shoji screens helped separate the space into more distinct areas.

"Sit, sit." Hikaru Himura gestured to the small table tucked into a tiny alcove with a mural painted to look like it was an outdoor patio.

He grabbed a pitcher of juice and joined her at the table while her mother busied herself at the cooktop.

Her dad poured them a drink and sat down.

"So..."

Naomi pursed her lips. "So."

"Melvin's place is in the Bihoro neighborhood," the parts store proprietor had told them.

Standing in the Bihoro neighborhood common area, Jax looked around. "Why am I not surprised this isn't one of the nicer neighborhoods?"

Kori nodded her agreement. The Bihoro neighborhood was not as well maintained as some of the other neighborhoods that Jax and Kori had passed through. The walkways had several cracks in the permacrete and more than one overhead light panel had burned out. Several of the torii gates at the tunnel entrances were gone or damaged.

"Sketchy neighborhood, check," Kori said. She turned to Jax. "Life with you is never boring."

"You're welcome," he said, grinning. After looking at the notes he'd taken as the old woman in the scrap shop gave them directions, he looked up and pointed. "Think it's that way."

The common space had six residential tunnel openings arrayed around the perimeter, in addition to the much larger tunnel that connected Bihoro to the next nearest neighborhood. They headed off.

"Think Naomi's doing okay? With her parents?" Kori asked.

Jax shrugged. "I dunno. Probably. She's tough."

Kori looked at him sideways. "You really are bad at being a human sometimes."

Jax made a sour face. "What?"

"I'll give a buy, given your history, but most people's parents don't send them away to mysterious Imperial boarding schools."

"Well, sure..."

"Never mind." She pointed. "I think that's it. Yeah?"

Jax checked his notes, confirming the residence number.

Melvin's door was faded and scarred. Jax could make out a few faded Kanji characters, but had no idea what they said. He tapped a message into his gPhone and hit send. The pair moved off to the side a few doors down from Melvin's place, taking up positions to look like travelers stopping to chat.

Two minutes later, Melvin's door swung open and an old man hobbled out, assisted by a cane.

"Our perp," Kori drawled.

"Big Fudge, the master criminal," Jax said.

The man hustled toward them, passing without a word. Kori watched him go, then said, "Let's go burgle a burglar."

The pair made their way toward their target. The upside of this neighborhood being not so desirable: folks did not loiter in the hallways. No one else was out and about.

Jax kneeled by the door handle. He looked up at Kori. "Keep an eye out." She nodded, rolling her eyes. There wasn't another soul anywhere in sight. He got to work. At times like this, Naomi's special gift really came in handy. Not that he hadn't broken into plenty of places before the two of them met.

He pulled up a few gray market apps on his gPhone. Shise was an older colony. The locking mechanism did not look like it had seen a firmware update since the founding of the colony. That was good news.

"Are you two getting to know each other?" Kori asked, looking down at Jax. "Hurry the hell up."

"You can't pressure gre—"

"Boy, I said hurry."

Jax frowned and focused on his phone screen. The software had connected to the door's locking system and was busy brute forcing its way through decades old security software.

Kori was about to needle Jax again when the door beeped. She looked around to confirm they were still alone in the wide corridor.

Jax looked up at her, pushing the now-unlocked door inward. He winked. "After you."

Melvin's living quarters were a hoarder's wet dream. Boxes, tablets, and paper manuals for who knew what made the narrow entry hallway even more narrow.

"Crap. How're we gonna find what we're looking for in all this?" Jax moaned.

Kori held her hands apart. "Well, we know they're this big, and ol' Fudge took four of them." She looked around. Then pointed to a corner of the living room. "That looks promising." She headed off toward the corner of the room where several boxes large enough to hold binary phase coils were stacked nearly to the ceiling.

Jax looked around. "Man, Melvin is hella sloppy."

"Are you looking for the things we're here to steal?" Kori snapped.

Jax stumbled and headed for the kitchen, where several boxes more or less the right size sat on the countertop.

After a few minutes, Kori shouted. "Got 'em!" She held up a piece of equipment that looked a lot like the picture Jax had on his gPhone.

Jax turned, smiling. The front door opened. His eyes grew wide. Kori turned to him, murder in her eyes. He looked around, his gaze settling on a closet behind Kori. He rushed over to her, pushing her toward the potential hiding place. Giving a silent prayer it wasn't full to capacity with Melvin's random crap, he opened the door.

"I could have sworn I locked that," Melvin mumbled, stepping out of the hallway. He hung his cane on a hook and surveyed the living room. "Where is that damn...There you are!"

In the closet, Kori was still glaring at Jax. "Why didn't you lock the door?" She hissed. In the tight space, he tried to shrug. "Move. Your. Hand." The closet had just enough room for the two of them, so long as they pressed their bodies together.

He made a face. "Sorry." There weren't many better places he could move his hand to, but he did his best.

Outside the closet, they heard Melvin rummaging around and mumbling to himself.

"He better not linger. This closet smells like feet," Kori growled.

Thankfully, Melvin found whatever he was looking for and shuffled back out the door.

After waiting two minutes, Jax eased open the door. "Clear."

CHAPTER 5

"This it?" Kori asked, adjusting the backpack with their free binary phase coil in it.

Melvin's ex-wife had been incredibly appreciative that they had been successful in liberating her merchandise from her grubby-fingered ex and that they'd done it so quickly. She happily handed over the coil with her best wishes and directions to the appropriate maglev station to get them to Naomi's parents' place.

Jax nodded. "This is the address she sent." He pressed the announcer button.

"At least it's a nicer neighborhood," Kori said, rocking on her heels. Jax nodded his agreement. His partner's parents had settled into what he assumed was one of the city's nicer and more well populated sections.

The door slid open. "Oh, thank God," Naomi exclaimed.

"Omi? Who's there?" a woman's voice called from inside the residence.

Naomi turned. "My friends, Mom." She turned back to

Jax. "You get the whatsit?" Jax nodded, pointing to Kori's backpack. She sighed. "Then it's time to go."

An older Japanese woman appeared behind Naomi. "Hello. Come inside." She pulled Naomi out of the way, ushering the two new guests into the residence.

Jax and Kori exchanged a look, the former stammering, "Actually ma'am, —"

Naomi's mother clucked, grabbing Kori's sleeve, pulling her in. Jax followed.

As they walked toward the living room, Jax and Kori behind them, Naomi's mother leaned in. "He's cute. Husband?"

"No, Mom."

Behind the two, Kori and Jax grinned.

"Boyfriend?"

"No," Naomi groaned.

Her mother looked over her shoulder at Kori. "Girlfriend?"

"Mom!"

The older woman held up both hands. "Sorry, sorry." She frowned. "You're not a nun, are you?"

Naomi threw her arms up. "Mom!" she sighed, pointing to her friends. "Mom. This is Jackson Caruso, my business partner, and Kori Lightning. A friend of ours. Guys, this is my mother, Kana Himura."

Jax held up a hand. "Hi."

Kori did the same. "A pleasure."

From the hallway that led to the bedroom, a voice shouted, "Who's here?"

Kana turned. "Omi's friends." She glanced at them. "None of them are her significant other."

Naomi's neck, then cheeks, burned. "Sweet boneless Christ." Her face fell into her hands.

Jax leaned toward Kori. "This is fun."

An older man appeared from the hallway. "I'm all packed." He had a lime green duffel bag in each hand. Spying the two new arrivals, he bowed. "Hello."

Naomi said, "Jackson Caruso, Kori Lightning. My father, Hikaru Himura."

Jax and Kori repeated their greetings, the former moving to take the bags from the other man.

"Thank you, young man." He looked to Naomi. "He's nice."

She rolled her eyes. "Can we please go?"

Her mother made a noise, drawing everyone's attention back to where she was standing in the kitchen area, a pitcher of juice in one hand, a stack of cups in the other. "Surely, we have a few minutes. Your friends just got here." She began arraying the empty cups to be filled.

Jax cocked his head. "We really should be going. Weren't you worried about the Imperials?"

"Yes, of course. They are why we called you, after all. But that was several days ago and, well, they don't seem to be that interested in bothering the colony, now." Kana smiled. "Besides, I'm not done packing."

Hikaru held up one of the lime green bags. "What's this, then?"

His wife clucked. "My dear sweet man." She nodded to the hallway. "Entertain the kids. I'll be out in a bit." She moved past her husband into the back room.

Hikaru Himura turned to the others. "So...Space adventurers?"

The group left the Himura residence and started back toward the spaceport. While the Imperial presence in orbit didn't seem to be causing an all-out panic, it wasn't a non-issue either. The chief topic of overheard conversations was the Empire.

As they progressed closer to the center of the Itabashi neighborhood, the number of people in the tunnels had grown considerably.

"Getting a little crowded," Kori said.

Jax nodded. He could only wonder what the Imperials had just done to stir the colonists up.

"The Empire will never let us rest!" Hikaru Himura hissed.

They reached a cavernous open space where four other large tunnels connected. Stalls lined the perimeter and formed several concentric smaller circles. The center featured a torii that looked like it was brought from Earth.

It was full of people. Lots of people.

"Oh, good. A party," Jax said. This wasn't great. From the tunnel he was pretty sure lead to the spaceport, six shock troopers and a naval officer stepped into the cavern. Well, that answered the "What did the Empire do to stir things up?" question. They landed troops. He growled to himself.

"Shit!" Kori hissed, pointing.

Naomi turned to her parents. "Is there another way to the port?"

Her mother nodded. She pointed to one of the other tunnels. "It'll take a bit longer, but we can go that way."

"Ladies, gentlemen, and those who identify as non-binary, may I have your attention!" the woman in the crimson Imperial Naval officer uniform shouted, for all the good it did. The crowd didn't notice. They were too busy talking and shouting amongst themselves.

Jax and company were almost at the tunnel when the officer tried again. "Ladies and gentlemen!" she shouted, louder than before. Being ignored again, she turned to one of the troopers and nodded.

The trooper took a step forward and raised their rifle to the cavern's ceiling. A single shot rang out.

It had the opposite of the intended effect. The crowd fell silent for a heartbeat, then erupted into chaos. The crowd surged first away from the Imperial Navy officers, then toward them.

Jax, Kori, and the Himuras reached the tunnel just as the crowd erupted in anger. The press of bodies rushed toward the group, separating them. Jax and Naomi caught sight of her parents and Kori making their way into the tunnel. "We'll meet you at the *Osprey!*" he shouted. Kori nodded and ushered the elderly couple deeper into the tunnel.

The shock troopers were pushing against the crowd, forming a wall, albeit not a big one, between the crowd and their superior officer.

Just as the crowd was parting enough for Jax and Naomi to follow the others, one of the shock troopers decided to try the shooting-into-the-air thing again.

The crowd wasn't impressed. In a single motion, the crowd overwhelmed the seven Imperials, cutting Jax and Naomi off from the tunnel they wanted.

He grabbed her arm. "This way." They fled down a tunnel that he hoped at some point either connected to the one the others took or led to the spaceport.

"If this leads to another shady ass old woman..." Jax said

as they jogged past citizens making their way toward the commotion.

"I'm sorry, what?" Naomi asked.

"Long story." Jax shook his head and headed for an intersection, a directory planted right in the center. "This is why I hate underground colonies." He jabbed the pulsing red YOU ARE HERE, then traced his finger along a route that looked like it would hit the tunnel Naomi's parents and Kori took a few hundred meters from the spaceport's entrance.

"This way," Kori said as she and the elderly Himuras stepped into the main concourse of the spaceport. It was unnervingly quiet and devoid of people. Kori looked around. There was an Imperial shuttle parked in the center of the floor directly under the wide circular opening in the top of the dome. *That would explain the troopers out at the main entrance. Glad these two knew about the service entrance*, she thought.

Mr. Himura gestured to the massive dome filled with ships. "Which is yours?"

Kori scanned the space, spotting the *Osprey*. She pointed. "That one."

Kana cooed. "Oh, that pretty red one?"

Kori shook her head. "Next to it."

"Ohhh."

"Nope. Other side."

"Oh."

"Yeah. But he has it where it counts. Trust me."

"He?" Hikaru asked.

Kori shrugged. "The SI identifies as male. His name is Skip."

He turned to her. "SI?"

Kori looked around, then remembered no one was around. She nodded.

"Intriguing."

From somewhere nearby, someone shouted, "Hey! You there!"

Kori's eyes went wide. She turned to the two Himuras. "Let me do the talking." She turned toward the voice to find a pudgy naval officer flanked by a pair of shock troopers stepping out of the Imperial shuttle. She swore under her breath. The shuttle had looked unoccupied. Clearly it was not.

He waved a tablet at Kori. "What're you doing?"

She looked around the bay. "Uh. Leaving?"

He made a face. "Did you not hear that the spaceport is off limits? For the safety and security of the people of Shise, all in and outbound traffic is suspended."

Kori opened her mouth but was cut off by Kana. "Our daughter is taking us off-world for one last time." She affected a sad face. "We're dying."

The officer raised an eyebrow. "Both of you?"

"Yes," Hikaru said.

The officer turned to Kori. "And she's your daughter?"

"Adopted. Obviously," Kana retorted.

"Uh, huh. And the luggage?" He pointed to the pair of lime green duffels.

Kori clucked. "Well, they ain't dying tomorrow." She leaned forward and made a face. "You gonna make 'em die here in the spaceport?"

The officer looked at each of his escort troopers in term. "Very well. Get to your ship. Get out of here." He waved a dismissive hand, turning to the troopers. He turned back. "Oh, and I'd hurry. The *Agamemnon* is enroute. Once she arrives, no one is getting on or off this planet."

Kori nodded. "Thanks." She started guiding the two Himuras toward one of the personnel lifts that ran along the inner surface of the dome, connecting the two landing levels. "Come on...Mom and Dad." The trio hurried off.

The stout officer watched them go, then turned to his escort. "Let's go get an inventory from space control. Oh, and call over to the Morriston landing party, get their manifest as well."

"Yes, sir," one of the troopers replied.

"There they are." Jax pointed to Kori and Naomi's parents stepping into the lift at the far end of the dome.

"Thank God," Naomi said, releasing a breath she didn't realize she'd been holding. "Come on."

They crept around the edge of the dome, doing their best to keep ships and equipment between them and the Imperial shuttle sitting in the middle of the bay.

"Weird no one is here," Naomi whispered.

Jax nodded. "Yeah. I guess everyone is too afraid to try and leave." The tunnel they'd followed had turned out to be a decommissioned secondary service access. Colony personnel had marked it closed, but, based on the various crates they'd seen along the way, were using it to store contraband.

"Think they'll do what they did at Jericho, here?" Naomi asked.

Jax shook his head. "No way. Jericho is one thing, but a

whole colony? An Imperial one? No way." He met her gaze. "Right?"

She shook her head. "I'd have agreed if Jericho hadn't just happened."

They reached a lift opposite the one Kori and the Himuras had taken. The *Osprey* was parked somewhere along the upper level between the two lifts.

After boarding the lift, she said, "The Empire is thrashing around a lot. I think our mutual friend is getting to them."

Jax nodded. "And a lot of innocent people are paying the price."

The lift arrived at Level 2. "At least whatever they're doing here, they're not ready to lock it down yet," Jax said. He spotted the familiar blue Valerian Co-Op Infiltrator and pointed. "Come on."

They were just passing a Jepsen Aero DX-34 when a commotion rang out below. Jax leaned out to look down and saw hundreds of people rushing into the port. He turned to Naomi. "Guess we were just early."

The crowd below was shouting and screaming, and once inside the dome, broke into groups streaming for every parked ship.

"Better hurry before this place goes full shit storm," she said.

Jax nodded and hurried past the Jepsen. The *Osprey* was three ships away. He spied Kori and the Himuras waiting for them at the foot of the boarding ramp. The old couple waved when they caught sight of Naomi. She broke into a run, taking them both into her arms.

Jax reached them and gave Kori a fist bump. He held up the binary phase coil. "Let's get this done and get the hell out of here." She nodded her agreement. He turned to Naomi. "Get your folks squared away."

She guided her parents up the boarding ramp. Kori watched them go, then asked Jax, "You know what to do with that?"

He looked at the binary whatsit. "Nope." He shrugged. "Skip will. He can walk me through it."

One of the ships down on the main level exploded. Screams came from the crowd, followed by the sounds of plasma rifles firing.

They looked at each other. "Time to go!" they said as one before rushing up the ramp.

"Skip. What do I do with this thing?" Jax shouted, holding the binary phase coil up for the ship's SI to see in one of the cargo hold cameras.

"Take it to the equipment bay."

"You mean the hump."

"I am not referring to it as a hump. It is on me. I do not have a hump."

Jax reached the common deck. "If the hump quacks."

"It does not, because it is not a hump. I do not have a hump."

Jax chuckled and headed aft to the hallway that ran along the starboard side of the ship leading to the crew berths. Rungs that normally laid flat to keep the corridor clear popped into place as a hatch overhead slid open.

The equipment bay was cramped and hot. Jax hated it, but it was where the Valerian Co-Op ship builders placed most of the ship's sensitive gear, namely the wormhole generator and ancillary equipment. Skip assured him that the hump's hull plating was extra thick. It wasn't as reassuring as the SI thought it was.

"Okay, where to?" Jax could feel the sweat forming on his brow already.

"The polarity management array on the starboard side. The panel is open."

From the same speaker, Rudy said, "Several ships on this level are powering up. Two from the ground level have departed. The Imperials are calling in reinforcements to pacify the spaceport."

Jax crawled to the polarity management array and reached inside. He felt around for a minute. "Ah, there we go." He withdrew his hand, clutching the burned-out doodad. He dropped the damaged coil and slotted the new one inside the machine.

After a moment, Skip said, "That did it."

Jax closed the whatever-Skip-had-called-it and crawled out of the hump as fast as he could.

The deck shook as he stepped off the ladder, the rungs folding back into the wall, the overhead hatch sliding closed.

Jax reached the bridge as a mid-size personal transport that had been parked next to them flared its lift engines, making its way toward the dome's opening.

"Preflight checks are complete," Skip announced.

CHAPTER 6

"Incoming hail," Skip announced. "All channels."

The overhead speaker beeped. "Attention citizens of Shise. By order of the Emperor, your colony is under lockdown. All spaceports are closed, effective immediately."

Kori and Naomi came up onto the bridge. "That sounded bad," the latter said.

Jax nodded. "Your parents good?"

Naomi took her seat. "Yeah, they're interrogating Baxter."

Kori grabbed hold of Rudy's station. "Poor guy."

Jax watched as another ship, a rusty-looking microfreighter flying the New Terra flag, rose on uneven lift engines. He gave the *Osprey*'s own lift engines power, rising to follow the larger vessel out of the dome. With luck, they could stay in its shadow all the way out of orbit. He wasn't sure why the Empire had waited to affect a lockdown but was glad they had and didn't plan to stick around to find out.

As the *Osprey* rose up and out of the Ny Hokkaido

Spaceport dome, the pale blue outline indicating the static atmosphere barrier passed harmlessly by.

"Bank left," Skip said. Jax obeyed without a second's hesitation. Outside the bridge window, a small personal yacht shot up from behind and below, its lift engines glowing white hot as the craft fought for altitude.

Jax adjusted their course, deciding that with so many ships making mad dashes to orbit, one more wouldn't stand out. He pushed the lift engine throttle all the way forward while pushing the main atmospheric engines up to full power. The *Osprey* roared as it overtook the freighter and closed on the offensive little personal yacht that nearly collided with them.

"An Imperial corvette is overhead and powering up its weapons," Skip announced.

"Not good," Kori said from the back of the bridge.

Bright green bolts of energy lanced through the clouds, stabbing into the small yacht, blowing holes right through it before it exploded.

"Karma," Jax whispered, pushing the *Osprey* out of the path of the falling debris.

"Activating all countermeasures," Skip announced, then added, "Launching decoys." Two loud pops echoed through the ship as two panels along the *Osprey*'s dorsal section slid open to allow decoy drones to launch.

More Imperial weapons' fire rained down, scattering the dozens of ships in the sky near the *Osprey*. Each volley of energy blasts lit up the sky with a sickly green light.

Jax juked the flight controls this way and that, doing his best to keep the ship on an outbound trajectory while not being an easy-to-hit target.

Down on the common deck, the two elder Himuras were sitting on the couch looking up at Baxter, who stood nearby, his feet magnetized to ensure that Jax's wild maneuvering didn't send him flying across the room.

"So, this is a new body?" Kana asked.

Baxter nodded. "Yes. When we were aboard the *Goliath*, I was damaged and dying." Both of them gasped. He went on. "There were hundreds of droids on board and they realized I was losing functionality. They brought me to one of the ship's droid foundries. There were many droid frames like mine. The ship transferred my processing core to one of them."

Hikaru shook his head. "That's incredible." He leaned forward. "So, you're now effectively restored back to factory new? New parts. No wear and tear or degradation." Baxter nodded. "Outstanding."

The ship rocked, and it sounded like something in one of the crew berths fell to the deck.

"Oh, my!" Kana Himura exclaimed.

Baxter tilted his head. "Do not worry. That was someone else exploding." He moved his head to make it seem like he was making eye contact with each of them, something Skip said was reassuring to humans. "Nearby."

The elderly woman shook her head. "That is not reassuring."

From the overhead speaker, Jax announced, "Hold onto something."

Up on the bridge, Jax threw the *Osprey* into a tight spin, letting Skip eject jammers that spat out metallic confetti and wide spectrum EM pulses that wreaked havoc on targeting sensors.

Naomi looked at her screens. They were about to pass between two of the Imperial ships. With luck, their jammers and the dozen or so surviving ships that made it out of the atmosphere with them would be enough cover for the *Osprey* to reach a safe distance from the planet to open a wormhole.

The two corvettes were firing blindly. They were lucky that the *Osprey* wasn't the only ship equipped with less-than-legal countermeasures.

The ship rocked more than once. Something over Rudy's station erupted in sparks. A metallic squeal came from somewhere down on the common deck.

"Almost there!" Jax hissed between clenched teeth. The lights on the bridge dimmed briefly.

"Rerouting power to shields," Skip informed.

"I have a course plotted," Rudy said. To be heard over the general rumbling of the ship, he increased the volume of his vocalizer.

Jax swung the ship into another tight turn, turning it into a corkscrew that carried them past the two small warships.

"Yes!" He pumped a fist. Reaching for the wormhole generator panel, he flipped a switch cover and powered up the device. The indicator on the panel began to pulse orange, the generator building up enough charge to open the rift in space-time.

"An Adjudicator class starship just popped in!" Naomi shouted.

The indicator flicked from orange to green. "Just in time." He slapped the activation trigger. Directly ahead of the *Osprey*, an orange and purple rip appeared directly ahead of them.

"Young man, this ship is disgusting, especially your restroom," Kana Himura said once everyone was together on the common deck.

The *Osprey* was rocketing through the wormhole, putting Shise and the Imperials as far behind them as possible.

After their escape and confirming that nothing important had been damaged, everyone turned in for the night, grabbing ration bars on their way to their rooms.

Naomi wrinkled her nose. "I've been telling him that since we met."

Kori raised a hand. "Me too."

Jax had his back to the group as he shoved the last of the eggs from the refrigerator around the hot skillet. He looked over his shoulder at the two women, then the elderly Japanese couple. "You all are welcome to clean it, or walk the rest of the way to..." He looked around. "Rudy, where are going?"

"Gael," the droid replied from across the room. He was sitting in his charging cradle next to the bulkhead-mounted entertainment display.

"Gael?" Hikaru repeated. "I'm not familiar with it."

"It seemed like a safe place to collect ourselves. It will take three days to reach, and is far enough out that we should not encounter any Imperials," the droid offered.

Jax turned his attention back to breakfast. "Thanks. Gael is as good a layover spot as any place." He shrugged. "I think. Never been." He turned, skillet in hand, depositing a serving of eggs on every plate.

Kori smiled. "What's not to like? Dudes in skirts." Her grin turned more wolfish. "Usually commando."

Naomi groaned. "Kor..." She glanced at her parents,

both of whom affected the sweetest of smiles, which only made her cheeks warm even more.

Jax grabbed the plate of bacon he was keeping warm in the small oven. "Here we go."

The only table on the common deck was the small three-person table affixed to the starboard bulkhead. Naomi and her parents were at the table while Kori and Jax's plates were on the coffee table in the lounge space on the other side of the room.

"So," Naomi said, looking at her mom and dad. "Why now?"

Hikaru put his fork down. "What do you mean, why now?" He cocked his head to the right, studying his daughter.

She stared at him. "What do you mean, why now? What?" She set her own utensil down, looking from parent to parent. "Why, after all these years, did you call me? We haven't spoken or seen each other since I was a preteen."

"We..." her mother started, but a sob cut her short. She inhaled. "Omi. We were told you were dead. That you'd been killed in a maglev accident. You'd tried to stowaway. That you slipped and fell under the train." She couldn't hold back the tears this time. Her husband put his arm around her.

Naomi squinted. "And you believed them? After they moved us to Terra Nova? After those Imperial handlers of yours asked all about me? After that, you just accepted that I ran away from the mysterious program you couldn't know anything about?"

Her father's face scrunched up. "Of course not. Omi, we never believed, but what could we do? The Emperor himself was overseeing our project. We couldn't trust the others on our team and we were under constant scrutiny by the security services."

His words made perfect sense to Naomi, but she was too deep in the rage and pain that she had until now kept carefully bottled up. "Then why now? You've obviously been happy without me all this time. Why contact me now?"

Her mother snuffled and looked at her daughter. "We didn't know what else to do." At the confused look Naomi gave her, she continued, "We ran. Omi, we ran when we realized what he was having us be a part of. We didn't know what else to do," she repeated.

Hikaru picked up the explanation. "If the Imperials sifted the colony's records too deeply, our forged identities would stand out. We didn't have the time or resources for IDs that would hold up too much scrutiny."

"You didn't change your names," Naomi said.

Her father scoffed. "We like our names. We changed our biographies. We figured Shise was too unimportant to ever attract Imperial attention. Everyone paid their taxes."

Her mother added, "There were also a lot of Himuras there."

Naomi nodded. "And if they figured out you were deserters..."

Her parents nodded.

Her mother said, "But we never stopped looking for you. After you disappeared, we hired a private investigator. Many of them. Most never found anything, likely because of Imperial intelligence's meddling. We settled here eight years ago after a scare about our identities. We hired another investigator. She found a few traces here and there. Enough to convince us that the Empire had lied. When she discovered records for some Imperial program you were in as a child, she refused to keep looking. But we knew then that you were out there. That we'd been misled. A year ago, another investigator came across your details tied to a business license on Kelso station."

Naomi sat in silence. So many of the questions that had haunted her for years, that she thought she'd successfully banished, had resurfaced and been answered.

Her mother reached across the small table. "Why didn't you find us?"

The question struck Naomi like a kick to the stomach.

On the other side of the room, Jax and Kori exchanged a look.

Naomi shook her head. She hadn't faced that question before. She'd never asked herself that question. It was just how it was. She cleared her throat. "I...They..." Her dad added his hand to his wife's on Naomi's arm. "They told me if I ever reached out to you, that you'd be punished. Killed." Tears fell down her cheeks.

Jax and Kori scarfed the rest of their breakfast down, the former saying, "You know, I think I need to check on...something, up on the bridge."

Kori nodded her head. "Oh, you need help? Happy to help. Let's go."

The pair leaped from the sofa and, as casually as possible, bolted for the staircase.

Naomi silently watched them go up the spiral stairs. She turned back to her parents. "I didn't want them to kill you and thought you didn't care about me."

Up on the bridge, the orange and purple swirling light of the wormhole cast the small space in dazzling colors. Jax spun his seat around to face the back of the bridge. Kori was sitting with her feet up on Naomi's console. "How long do you think we need to stay up here?"

She shrugged. "Skip, are they still talking?"

"Yes."

"Longer than this," she answered, smirking at Jax. "Shoulda grabbed some bacon on our way." He nodded his agreement.

Jax looked around the bridge, realizing he should have suggested the cargo deck. Someplace a bit less close-quarters. Sighing, he said, "So..." Why was this so awkward? He and Kori were friends. He looked to his right out the window. "How're things?"

"Things?" She quirked an eyebrow.

"You know: life, love, Jericho?" He blushed immediately as the last word left his mouth. "Sorry. Have you heard from your boss or friends and coworkers?"

She shook her head. "No worries, man. I haven't really processed it myself." She closed her eyes. "And no. I assume the rest of the team didn't get off the station. They were with Alfonse near his ship. I'd have heard if he or they got out. He's rich, so I assume he's okay. He's probably fuming at being cut off from the Internex." She looked at him. "Why do you ask?"

He shrugged. "I dunno. Friends ask about each other's lives, right? I know you and Naomi talk, but we," he pointed to her, then himself, "haven't in a while. You never come by Kelso anymore." He realized it sounded like an accusation. He felt his cheeks flushing.

She scrutinized him, finally answering, "They do. You don't, but I see you trying." She smiled. "Friends-wise?

Outside work, I don't really have that many friends on Jericho. Even after all this time, it just doesn't feel like home. Not like Kelso did."

Jax nodded, unsure of what else to say. It wasn't like he could criticize on the friends front. Outside of Naomi and Lucas, he wasn't sure who else he might count as a friend on Kelso station. And it wasn't like he ever saw Lucas outside the Angry Spacer, so maybe they weren't quite friends...He shook his head. He supposed he had the Delphinos too. That made him shudder.

She asked, "So. What about you? How's life, love?" She made a rolling motion with her hand. "You know."

Jax copied a gesture he'd seen his aunt make all his life, a kind of head nod and shake at the same time. "Well, you know we're doing shit work to keep the lights on because we did the right thing, or whatever, and got BioTek on our asses."

"Nasty habit you've developed. Doing the right thing." The last job Kori had done with Jax, they'd been hired to rob an ore shipment train on a backwater colony. When they discovered that the guy who hired them was part of the Crimson Orchid crime syndicate, they returned the ore and arranged for their client's goons to be arrested. The Crimson Orchid hadn't been happy.

Jax gave her a look, then nodded. "I blame Naomi."

Kori laughed. "More time to find someone to settle down with."

"Settle down? No thank you," he grinned.

"Some things never change," she replied with a smile.

"You?" He leaned forward.

She shook her head. "On again, off again with Marshall, but nothing serious. He stops by Jericho whenever he and Steve are in the area." She made a face. "That man will make a good husband someday. I just don't know if I have the patience to wait for him to get there."

Jax clucked. "I still don't know what you see in that big idiot."

She gave him a look. "The same thing you saw in his brother." She waved off whatever his reply was going to be. "He's a good guy. You got weird Delphino baggage."

"No, I don't."

Kori rolled her head on her neck. "My man. You three hated each other in school, then you went and slept with one of them. Then broke up with him." She smirked. "That doesn't even address the time in Steve's life you two got involved." She clucked. "That's baggage."

"Whatever." He made a face. "Steve's a good guy. He's settled into his life pretty well." He shrugged. "As far as I know. They're off-station more often than not these days. Haven't seen them in a few months." He shrugged again. "He was dating an old dude. Kinda hot, but still a definite age difference. I think that ended."

She nodded. "Yeah, last time Marshall and I spoke, he mentioned they'd picked up a steady contract hauling supplies for someone. He was pretty cagey about the who."

Jax smiled. "Good for them. I don't hate not seeing Marshall's ugly mug at the Spacer or Wendy's."

Changing the subject, Kori asked, "What about you two...or four? What've you all been up to? I mean, other than wreaking havoc across half the Empire while being chased by a definitely-not-legally-armed corporate warship." She shuddered, remembering the news coverage of that VP guy's trial. On his orders, hundreds of people died. The trials of those who followed his orders had been tough to watch. How Jax and Naomi had kept their names out of it was beyond her. Jackson Caruso luck.

"Heard about that, huh?" Jax asked. As proud as he was of what they'd done, he was trying to not attract any corporate hit teams.

She clucked. "Man, the whole Empire heard about that. You're lucky Skip is so good at disguising his identity. And yours." Valerian Co-Op Infiltrators were rare, but not so rare that anyone knowing the details would think it was Jax.

He nodded. "Yeah, we've been lying low, just in case."

"Good call. I know they arrested a bunch of other execs, and that one guy, Sanchez, he's gonna die on a penal colony, but yeah, I doubt BioTek's board, what's left of them, will forget about you anytime soon."

"I am unforgettable."

"Calm down, tiger," she said, rolling her eyes. "How do you think Naomi is doing?" Her concern was plain on her face. The two had bonded when the other woman teamed up with Jax, mostly against his will, and they all went on a grand adventure that turned out to be robbing innocents on behalf of a criminal syndicate.

Jax shrugged. "You know. I don't know. Since I've known her, she's been all tough and no family, lone wolf woman." He chuckled. "Granted, that span is all of two years." A shrug. "We'll see." He made a face. "Does that make sense? Lone wolf woman?"

"They have finished their discussion. Naomi is in her quarters with Rudy," Skip announced.

Kori looked at Jax. "With Rudy?"

"Who the hell knows?" He shrugged.

"For the record, no, that doesn't make sense," Kori added.

"I should have just ignored the message," Naomi said. She was in her berth with Rudy. The conversation had died in awkward silence. She fled to her berth. Her parents went down to the cargo deck.

Rudy's large optical sensor spun, whirring as he focused on her. "Your vitals have been elevated since you came aboard."

"Since they came aboard," she corrected.

Rudy made a honking sound. "A distinction without difference right now. You cannot maintain this level of stress indefinitely."

She looked at the droid. "Why are you here again?" Rudy had followed her to her berth.

He made his best approximation of a shrug. "I thought you might need someone to talk to."

She shook her head. "This is weird."

He held up a small fist, bobbing it up and down—the best he could approximate a nod. "Did your conversation over breakfast help?"

She shrugged. "It's a start. This is just..." Another shrug. "A lot. I think I need some space, ease into this. At least they'll be gone soon. A little distance might help."

Rudy let out a soft whistle. "Will they? Be gone soon? It is unlikely we can leave them at Gael. That will mean that they will likely accompany us back to Kelso station. From there, it is anyone's guess how long it will take them to find new lodgings. Assuming, of course, they do not simply choose to take up residence on the station." His optical array whirred and clicked. "Your vitals have spiked, again."

Down on the cargo deck, Baxter was entertaining the two elderly Himuras. He deployed one of his shoulder-mounted railguns, letting it track around as he moved.

"Incredible," Hikaru said. "Your railgun can track entirely separate from your main combat functions?"

"Correct," the big matte black droid replied. He deployed both forearm blasters. "I can track up to eight targets at once, prioritizing them three at a time."

Kana, sitting on a bench near the starboard cargo door, said, "We'd heard so much about combat droids during the war but never saw them."

Her husband nodded. "The fighting never made it close enough to us."

"Count yourselves lucky," Baxter said. "When I was aboard the *Goliath,* I accessed the collected logs from several battles. It was...unpleasant."

Hikaru cocked his head. "You didn't fight?"

Baxter shook his head. "Briefly, in the early days. I protected the Carusos for a time until they left me on Kelso station to keep Jackson safe." He paused. "It was the last time I saw Thomas and Allison Caruso."

Both Himuras nodded slowly. "A noble assignment. We're sorry."

Baxter nodded his agreement. "I was angry about it at the time, but in hindsight, would not trade the assignment, or the experiences that followed, for anything."

Kana looked up at Baxter. "You are possibly the most sensitive droid I've ever met."

"Don't tell anyone." He turned his head. "Or I'll kill you."

Her eyes went wide.

"Kidding." At a much lower volume, he added, "Not kidding."

The *Osprey*'s bridge was crowded before picking up the two extra Himuras. Adding them to the group had made it downright cramped. Naomi's parents and Kori were all clinging to handholds at the rear of the small space.

Jax hoped one of them didn't go tumbling down the stairwell. "Local space in ten," he announced.

Kana leaned around her husband. "So, they all wear kilts?"

Kori shook her head. "I mean, I doubt everyone does. But from what I read on WikiGalaxia, it sure sounds like it's the predominate article of clothing." She rubbed her hands together. "I wonder how—"

"Down, girl," Jax said from up front. "Exiting wormhole." He reached forward and toggled the wormhole generator to open an exit. Directly ahead of them, the swirl of brilliant orange and purple exotic energies ripped apart; the black of space stood before them.

The *Osprey* shot out of the hole in space-time. The planet Gael was a small blue and green dot.

"Scanners active," Skip announced.

As they approached the planet, details in orbit came into focus. Several of the displays mounted around the small bridge showed the planet and what was in orbit around it. It formed a busy picture.

"Is that...?"

"The *Goliath*? Yes," Naomi said, her eyes glued to her console as she flicked through sensor data. "Plus a few other Nemesis Fleet ships."

From the back, Hikaru Himura asked, "Should we leave? Before they see us?"

Jax shook his head. "I doubt they care about us, but I'm also not sure where else we'd go. A few more days and we'll be eating ration packs I bought from a surplus dealer a few years ago."

"Gross," Kana Himura said.

Her daughter turned to her. "You don't know the half of it." She stuck out her tongue.

Jax nodded his agreement. "Down we go." He pushed the flight controls forward, guiding the *Osprey* toward the planet.

"I have space control flight guidance," Rudy said.

On Jax's console, one of the smaller displays flicked to tracking data showing the *Osprey*'s route and the route space control wanted them to take to one of the smaller spaceports of Aberdeen, Gael's coastal resort community. The familiar ghostly green arrow appeared on the heads-up display in front of him.

Kori watched as the massive and ancient warship increased in size. "What're they doing here?"

Naomi's dad whistled. "You all found that?"

Jax looked over his shoulder. "Sure did."

"And then gave it to the Resistance?" the older man added.

Jax faced forward, frowning. "Stupid Baxter." Naomi stifled her laughter, then turned to her parents and Kori. "We didn't have a lot of options at the time."

Her mother smiled. "The *Goliath* must have been an AI treasure trove."

"Still is," Naomi said. She smiled. "Tiny aggressive little vacuums."

Jax shuddered. "So many little vacuums. And mean."

Kori leaned forward. "What're they doing?"

"Who?" Jax asked without looking.

"Who do you think? The Resistance."

"The *Goliath* and her support craft are loitering in high orbit," Skip said.

"They hailing us?" Jax asked.

"Nope," Rudy replied.

"Any indication they've noticed us?"

"Nope."

"Good, then we're not messing with 'em." He adjusted their course, careful to stay within the guides the local space control authority sent up but putting as much distance as he could between them and the Resistance.

His thoughts drifted back to what should have been an incredibly lucrative score. The salvage even a few ships of the Nemesis Fleet would have brought in would have set him and Naomi up for life. The entire fleet...He shuddered.

"You okay up there?" Naomi asked.

"Oh. Uh...yeah." He shook his head. They'd been forced to give the few Nemesis Fleet ships they were able to access to the Resistance to keep them away from the scavengers that found the fleet. That stupid weirdo lieutenant and his shady partners ruined everything.

He scowled as the first plasma streamers began to form against the *Osprey*'s shields.

The planet Gael had been colonized in the later stages of the Phase Two colonial expansion, only a few years before the Unification War broke out. Much of the planet's land area was lush jungle, where it wasn't hilly highlands. A single ocean took up just under half the planet's surface, with several large cities along its shores.

Much of the colony's income came from the wealth of

exploitable sea life in that massive ocean, from microscopic organisms with pharmaceutical benefits to massive whale-like creatures that tasted delicious. Tourism made up the rest, and Jax could see why. From up high, the coastal cities looked downright luxurious, and the few smaller settlements he could see tucked into the jungles looked just as nice.

Turbulence rocked him out of his sightseeing. "Be down in a few. Better go settle in for landing."

Kori and the Himuras filed down the stairs. Rudy beeped, then said, "So, what is the plan?"

Jax glanced over his shoulder. "Well, we'll find someplace cheap to lie low for a few days, get some supplies." He frowned. "Sorry, you and Baxter are gonna have to stay aboard the ship. At least until we know where the locals fall on the topic of droids. Sorry." You never could tell where a colony stood on droids until you got out into the community. The last thing they needed was for Baxter or Rudy to draw an angry crowd.

Rudy emitted two sad beeps. "It is okay."

The Aberdeen Municipal Spaceport Three was a small non-cargo port on the south end of town on a bluff overlooking the Aengus sea. Several smaller vessels were coming and going, their lift engines roaring. With one eye on his guidance screen and another out the forward window, he brought the *Osprey* in around the spaceport in a nice low and slow turn.

Naomi stood up to look out the section of window nearest her console. "That's a nice spaceport."

From his side of the bridge, Rudy said, "And this is the third-tier spaceport."

"How do you know this isn't just, you know, the third one they built?" Jax asked.

Naomi sighed. "Does it matter?"

Jax brought the *Osprey* in toward their assigned landing pad. "I've already forgotten what we were talking about."

Down on the common deck, Kori draped herself over the large chair. "So, how're you two doing? You know, with Naomi and everything?"

Kana and Hikaru, seated on the sofa, exchanged a look. The former said, "It's complicated." Her husband snorted. She elbowed him. Turning to Kori, she said, "Calling Omi was our last-ditch effort. We knew if the Empire set up shop and started digging through the colony's records, they'd spot our forged records. Even if they didn't know who we were, really, they'd know we had forged idents and come sniffing around."

Hikaru chimed in. "We didn't have anyone else to call. Believe us, this wasn't how we wanted to reconnect with Omi."

Kori nodded. "Well, as maybe her only other friend besides Jax—and well, he's Jax. Give her time. I don't know much about her life other than that she met Jax on Mariposa. She was working as a relief worker. She never told me why."

Both Himuras nodded their understanding.

PART 2

CHAPTER 7

The *Osprey* settled on her landing gear with a groan. Release valves in the landing gear bays hissed, releasing steam. The boarding ramp lowered.

Jax was the last one to step off the ramp. He took a deep breath, inhaling the salt air. "Wonder what real estate is like here?"

Kori made a face. "You already forget about the neighbors?" She pointed up.

Jax pursed his lips. "Good point." He waved to the spaceport's exit. "Come on. I'm hungry. I say grab lunch, then we can do some shopping, stock up the ship." He pointed to the three Himuras. "You three can find us lodgings and work on your family stuff."

Kori rolled her eyes. "Smooth."

They made their way out of the spaceport and found a public transit terminal just outside.

"Well, I'll be," Hikaru Himura said. He pointed. "A funicular."

Jax looked first at him, then to where he was pointing. A weird-looking train was creeping its way up the side of the bluff along a narrow track that ran down to the city below. He blinked a few times. "What the hell is that?"

"Funicular," Hikaru repeated.

Jax turned. "Oh. Sorry. I thought that was an exclamation, like 'jinkies.'"

The other man rolled his eyes as he rubbed the back of his neck.

The funicular arrived and disgorged passengers before an automated voice said, "Please board the train."

"How polite," Kana said as she led the way onto the vehicle. Just before the vehicle's doors closed, a trio of spacers jumped on. They smiled at the group before turning to continue whatever conversation they were having before realizing they needed to run or they'd miss their ride down to the city and have to wait for the next. Hikaru's gaze was fixed out the window, taking in the scenery.

Jax was looking at his gPhone as they descended toward Aberdeen proper. The city below spanned several kilometers, mostly a narrow strip a kilometer wide following the sea's coastline. The downtown core was a dozen or two glass and steel towers that reached hundreds of stories, topping out higher than the bluff the team was leaving. Several had private landing pads at their tops.

"Now arriving. Please hold on to handrails until the vehicle comes to a stop," the funicular car said in its pleasant, slightly accented voice. Everyone filed out.

Jax held up his gPhone. "How's Paco's sound?" The others all leaned in to look at the menu on his device's screen, nodding their agreement. He smiled. "Let's go."

Naomi fell in next to Kori. "As long as it's not all eels." The other woman shuddered, then chuckled her agreement.

"Eels?" her father asked. Naomi slowed, falling back with her parents. Kori smiled, hearing Naomi start the story of how she came to meet Jax and Kori. Smiling, she sped up to catch up to Jax, giving the three Himuras some privacy.

Jax spied her next to him. "Is it weird that I'm super excited for a chimichanga?"

She looked at him. "Yes. Yes, it is."

They reached Paco's Seaside Taqueria somewhere between the lunch rush and happy hour, which worked out well. At least Jax thought so until the hostess, a young woman fresh out of secondary school, said it'd be a 45-minute wait.

Jax craned his neck to look past her. "There's lots of open seats."

She smiled a well-practiced and entirely insincere smile. "Sorry, sir, but not all sections are open right now."

Jax was about to say something when Kana Himura shoved past him. "Excuse me, you mean to tell me you'll make an elderly couple sit around for most of an hour?"

The hostess's smile faltered a moment. "I'm sorry, ma'am, but—"

"But nothing. In that time, he'll," she hitched a thumb over her shoulder toward her husband, "need to pee six times and I'll need a nap." She made a show of checking the time on her gPhone. "It's already nearing my afternoon nap time, and I need time to digest." She frowned, turning to Hikaru. She started speaking in Japanese, her tone shrill. He did a lot of shrugging and saying placating-sounding things back to her.

Jax pursed his lips and looked at the hostess, eyebrows arched as if to say, "Ball's in your court."

The hostess's iron demeanor cracked. "Actually, folks..." She held up a hand, hoping to catch Kana's eye. "I think I can get you seated."

Kana turned, her face placid. "On the patio. By the water."

The young woman nodded vigorously. "Of course." She grabbed a handful of thin digital flexiscreens. "This way."

As Kana walked past Jax, she winked. He turned to Naomi, who was beet red.

"That was the single best chimichanga I've ever eaten," Jax said, one hand rubbing his stomach. "I'm gonna have to see if Lucas can make those." Lucas was the proprietor of the Angry Spacer, Jax's favorite bar on Kelso station. His hamburgers were famous station wide.

He and Kori had excused themselves from the group's late lunch, or early dinner, to fetch supplies. It gave the three Himuras a chance to catch up over drinks while enjoying the scenery.

Kori, walking next to him, said, "It wasn't obvious the way you inhaled the thing, like it had the antidote."

"Whatever. You're just jealous. That tostada was looking a little lackluster."

She nodded her begrudging agreement. "It was." Looking at him, she added, "You know it was made of whale or whatever they call them here."

"What?"

She nodded. "Yup. I noticed it in the food allergy section on the back of the menu. All the meat dishes were," she snapped her fingers, "what's that they call them? Oh, whulls, that's right."

Jax thought about it a moment, then shrugged. "I can

see why export them. Tasty, tasty whulls." He made it a little song. She shook her head, smiling. "I'll have to talk to Lucas."

The pair were walking along the coastline pedestrian mall. One side of the boardwalk was stall after stall of food, artists, and novelty goods sellers. The other side was the expansive ocean and its gently rolling waves.

"If I was with anyone else, this would be romantic," Kori mused.

He turned. "Anyone else? I'm hurt. I'm romantic."

"Okay, Mr. Dating Apps." She spied a cab and stepped out into the street to flag it down. Turning to Jax, she asked, "Know where we're going?"

He held up his gPhone. "CostShaver. Four kilometers along the coast, then inland, almost to the jungle." He jumped into the cab behind her, shoving her further into the backseat. "Scoot," he urged.

"Where to?" the driver, an elderly woman with intricate gray-haired cornrows, asked.

"CostShaver," Jax said.

"I love your hair, ma'am," Kori said.

The woman looked over her shoulder. "I like your hairstyle, young lady."

Kori grinned at the compliment, reaching up to pat her hair.

Once they were underway, Kori turned in the seat. "You think you and the Delphinos will ever set things right?"

Jax made a face. "What do you mean? We're good." He cocked his head. "Aren't we?" Her look spoke volumes. "I mean, I totally cut them in on what we got for the Nemesis Fleet."

"To hear Marshall tell it, that was only after you left

them stranded and tried to take it all for yourself and felt guilty."

"Naomi woulda got a cut—" He saw her face and bit his lip. "Okay. I guess I see your point, but..." She gave him a flat, expectant look. "They said it was fine."

She shook her head. "I know you can be a human when you set your mind to it. Naomi told me about your," she lowered her voice, "messenger friend."

Jax's cheeks burned crimson. "That was a special case."

"Why? Because he was cute? You've known Marshall and Steve since elementary. I know you three have bickered and shit, but dude, come on. They've had your back."

"One, he wasn't that cute, or my type. Two, I...well...I thought I made it up to them!" Jax could feel his cheeks still burning and felt the back of his neck warming.

She shook her head. "The problem is you keep them at arm's length. Even on jobs." When he said nothing, she continued. "Naomi—"

"I don't like how close you two are. Am I the only topic of conversation?"

Her eyes narrowed. "Boy, please."

From the front of the vehicle, the driver said, "Here we are, you two." The cab pulled to a stop outside a sprawling shopping complex.

"Thanks." Jax hopped out.

As Kori was sliding to join him, the driver said, "Sister, he's a lot work."

"Girl, I know. Thankfully, he's not mine," she winked, paying the fare before she exited the vehicle.

The CostShaver was massive. Jax shook his head. "You know, I was in a fake one of these based on a place from Earth." He nodded toward the large warehouse. "This really isn't that far off." He held his hands as far apart as possible. "Was massive."

"Give me Spacer Wares any day," Kori agreed.

The warehouse was bright pink with a yellow horizontal stripe around the middle. The entry lobby way was floor to very-high-ceiling glass, filled with large potted plants. A greeter stood nearby, checking people in.

Outside the building, a few dozen protesters were marching back and forth. Their signs were variations on "Go Away, Empire."

Jax watched the group for a minute. "Pretty bold." He looked at Kori. "I've never seen anyone be so open about it."

She shook her head. "Usually not a very safe idea." She looked up at the sky. "Seems especially dangerous given..." She pointed. "You know."

Jax nodded, then said, "Maybe that's why they feel safe enough to be out here."

She nodded her agreement.

The pair checked in and provided the delivery details to make sure their purchases would arrive at the spaceport and the *Osprey*.

The clerk handed them a scanner. "Just scan and select the quantity you'd like. You can check out at any time on your scanner." She smiled.

Jax held out his hand. "Shall we?"

The Aberdeen Municipal Spaceport Three was oddly quiet, even for a smaller port. Skip was watching his passive sensors and camera feeds. After having Baxter, in his ridiculous cloak, sneak off the ship to attach the data umbilical, Skip was able to quickly hack his way into the spaceport's network, and from there, the network of all spaceports on Gael. Ship traffic had slowed since their arrival, but as far as he could tell, there was no alert or any sign that planetary space control authorities even knew the *Goliath* was up there just outside the planet's gravity well.

Do you think they do not know the Goliath *is up there?* Skip beamed to the other two SI's aboard the *Osprey*.

No way. They have to know it is up there, Rudy transmitted. *A ship that big is hard to miss.*

It is also not alone, Baxter reminded the other two.

In a separate conversation thread, Skip sent, *We should hire a gig worker to clean the bilge. The Captain will do a poor job of it, if he does it all.*

Agreed, Rudy sent. *I can supervise.*

An hour later, a young man was standing outside the *Osprey*. He looked at the raised boarding ramp. "Hello?" He had a bag full of gear slung over one shoulder.

The ramp lowered to the ground with a hiss. Rudy rolled down. "Hello."

The young man jumped. "Oh shit! A droid?" His eyes were the size of saucers. He looked around in case this was one of those candid vid shows.

"You're in no danger." Rudy held both hands up, palms out.

The man made a face. "I...uh...wasn't afraid of you. You're what? A meter tall?"

Rudy made an indignant sounding beep. "Anyway. Follow me." He rolled down the ramp. "We need to hook up the serving umbilicals before you get into the tank." He spun his head to look at the man. "You do have coveralls or something. Right?"

The man nodded. "Yeah, of course." He reached over his shoulder to pat the backpack he was wearing. "I'll need to change somewhere." He pointed to his blue and pink tartan kilt. "Coveralls don't go over kilts all that well."

Rudy bobbed on his smart material rollerball. "Okay. I will show you to the head." He headed up the ramp, the young worker following.

"This thing is in incredible shape," the young man said, taking in the cargo deck. "Most antiques aren't this well maintained."

"Excuse me?" the ceiling speakers said.

The man spun, startled. "Who? What?"

Rudy motioned him toward the central staircase. "Come on." He rolled into the open center and shot up to the common deck.

When the young worker reached the common deck, Rudy pointed. "Head is that way."

When the man emerged from the head in a bright orange jumpsuit, hood, and retracted face shield, Rudy emitted a series of beeps, pointing back down the stairs.

When the pair rolled and stepped off of the boarding ramp, Rudy pointed. "Umbilicals are here. There. And there." He rolled as he pointed. "When those are connected, come back aboard." He didn't wait for the young man to answer, zipping back up the ramp. The odds of being seen and reported were low, but not zero. Every second off the ship was a risk. Worst case, if the young man outside ratted them out, Baxter and Rudy could hide in the hold and Skip would do his Rudimentary Intelligence thing.

A few minutes later, the young man came up the boarding ramp. "Hi, uh, droid guy?"

Rudy had been busying himself in the small computer

area in the aft section of the cargo deck just outside engi-neering. He rolled out into the cargo hold.

Skip, can you open the bilge access? he asked the ship wirelessly. A panel near the center of the hold popped open. *Thank you.*

"You're all hooked up." The worker nodded toward the section of deck plating that had popped free. "That the access?"

Rudy beeped twice. "That is it. The tools you need are in a rack just inside."

The young man slid the access panel aside and peered into the *Osprey*'s inner workings, in particular, her bilge tank. "Yo. Has no one ever cleaned this?" His hood and face shield deployed.

Rudy made a rumbling noise. "You might think that. Good luck." He rolled back into the small computer bay. He could hear the man swearing as he lowered himself into the disgusting soup. *We should make sure to tip him exorbi-tantly,* Rudy told Skip and Baxter.

Agreed. If nothing else, it may encourage the Captain to perform regular maintenance tasks more...regularly, Skip replied.

Baxter sent an emoji that was laughing so hard it was crying.

After watching Jax and Kori head off on their errand, Naomi and her parents headed for what was billed as the "Crystal Kilometer: Over 300 retail shops featuring local artisans and creators from around Gael, all under one amazing roof." So said the advertisement they'd seen.

The shopping center, for lack of a better term, was, if Naomi was being honest, spectacular. The entry was off the main promenade that Jax and Kori had started down, but the bulk of the structure quickly sank below the waves, extending out into the sea.

"Your friend wasn't kidding. So many men in skirts," Kana whispered to Naomi as they passed a scarf shop.

"They're kilts, Mom."

Her mother shrugged.

"This is pretty," Hikaru said, lifting an exquisitely cut crystal octopus.

Naomi joined him, smiling at the heavyset, kilt-wearing man sitting with his legs spread to an almost inhuman degree. "Very nice."

Her dad turned. "Want it?"

She shook her head. "I'm not twelve. But thank you." Smiling, she glanced at the vendor, careful to not look at his inappropriately short kilt, before heading to the next stall.

As they progressed further out to sea, more and more fish became visible through the crystal-clear roof. It had a coating of some sort that kept light from reflecting off it, so if you did not know any better, you'd think nothing stood between you and the sea above. It was a neat effect, Naomi admitted to herself.

As they moved through the shopping center, Naomi caught several pieces of conversation. The topic on most folks' minds appeared to be the Resistance fleet in orbit. So, they knew the Resistance was up there. Until then, she had assumed that maybe the *Goliath* and its support ships hadn't announced themselves. Clearly, that wasn't the case.

Pulling her parents aside, she said, "Have you noticed? People are talking about the Resistance ships in orbit. Like, a lot."

Her father nodded. "I noticed. Do you think it's safe to remain here?"

Kana turned to her husband. "The mall?"

Hikaru made a clucking noise.

Naomi looked around, deciding that it would be safer to continue walking the concourse. The shopping center extended a half kilometer into the sea before turning back toward the shore. Several of the larger sea creatures were swimming slow circles in the center of the crystal horseshoe.

"We're only going to be here long enough to get some supplies and make sure there's no heat on us after Shise," Naomi assured her parents.

The trio walked in silence for a bit until Kana asked, "Do you think Gael plans to secede?"

Her husband, voice low, said, "No way. They'd be idiots to try. Gael isn't exactly Terra Nova, but it's also very much not out on the fringe." He shook his head. "The Resistance can't think that they could hold this place."

Naomi shrugged. "As long as they wait a day or two, I don't care what these folks decide."

"You think they're foolish?" her mother pressed.

"To rebel? Sure. To want out from under the Empire? Of course not. I'm no fan of the Empire, but I've seen their big ships up close and personal and, well, I don't think the *Goliath* would last long. Certainly not against more than one." She sighed. "If it's one thing the Empire has, it's ships."

Before either of her parents could reply, speakers hidden somewhere in the support structure of the shopping center squelched. The three Himuras stopped and looked around.

"Attention, please. Attention, please. The Crystal Kilometer will be closing immediately. Please make your way to the exit as quickly as possible."

Naomi groaned. "I really shoulda seen that one coming." A second later, her gPhone beeped. A message from Aberdeen city emergency services: *Take Shelter.* "Shit."

CHAPTER 8

After what felt like eight hours, the front of the building was in sight once again. "I still think you'd look good in a kilt," Kori said as they rounded a corner, leaving an aisle that was packed with kilts of all sizes and patterns. Some were elaborate tartan designs, while others were single color canvas jobs with many pockets.

"Uh. No. Too breezy," Jax said.

"Wear underwear," she said. She rolled her eyes, remembering that particular quirk of his.

He shook his head. "Why would I start now?" He patted his legs. "I'm all for skirts, even utility skirts. I've got pockets and warm legs." He shrugged.

She sighed.

They rounded another corner, entering an aisle for portable power generators and batteries. Jax stopped in his tracks. "Who needs 300 mini batteries?" Before Kori could reply, he cocked his head. "Do you hear that?" He tilted his head in the other direction.

Kori stopped, lowering the scanner. "What is it, Lassie? Is that hapless little boy stuck in the well?"

He flipped her off.

Chuckling, she focused on listening to whatever it was that Jax was hearing. Her eyes shot wide open. "Is that a civic alarm?" It was faint, coming from outside the building.

Before Jax could answer, both of their phones screeched out an alert tone, startling both of them.

The overhead speakers crackled before a panicky voice came on. "Attention, uh... attention, customers. Please make your way to the front exit as...what? No...shush, I'm on the PA. Please make your way to the front exit immediately." Jax and Kori exchanged a look, assuming the announcement was done, when the speaker continued. "Oh. This is not a drill, thank you."

Jax tapped his gPhone to the scanner screen to access the payment portal. He looked at Kori. "I'm gonna be pissed if they don't deliver this stuff."

She grabbed his arm and pulled him toward the building's glass entry, joining the flow of increasingly panicked shoppers.

Jax and Kori followed the crowd as it funneled out of the CostShaver. He looked around. Customers were making their way to one of the mass transit stations nearby while others milled around conversing with the protestors they'd seen earlier, all of them anxiously looking to the sky.

Jax nodded toward a group of sky gazers. "What do you think they know that we don't?"

Kori clucked. "That a trick question?"

Jax glared at her but said nothing. He pulled his gPhone out of his pocket while he patted other pockets looking for the earpiece that paired with it. He had a feeling he'd need it. Finding it and securing it in his ear, he said, "Skip, what's going on?" After a moment, he looked at Kori. "You got any network?" He held his phone up, showing her the screen.

She consulted her own gPhone. "Nope." She looked up, meeting his gaze. "That's not good."

He nodded his agreement.

One of the protestors came over to them. "You two aren't from here, right?" she asked in the thick brogue of the natives of Gael.

It took Jax a second to parse what she'd asked. He nodded. "Yeah. What's going on?"

"Imperials," was her only answer. "You best get to your ship," she added.

The pair nodded and made their way to the mass transit terminal. "Guess we're getting back the old fashioned way," Jax said, merging into the crowd waiting for busses. The taxi app on his phone was useless without network access. It wasn't clear who had shut the planetary network down, the Imperials or the local authorities. The end result was the same: lots of panic and no information.

"Do you know which one we need?" Kori asked.

Jax frowned. "Well, crap."

A woman with fiery red hair standing nearby leaned over. "The route schedule is over there. Thankfully, they print it quarterly." She pointed to a laminated display showing route numbers and destinations. "It's organized by zone," she added. Below the timetables, a map of the city with each zone color coded and a "you are here" icon showed how far they had to go to get back to the spaceport.

"Thanks," Jax said.

As Jax moved off to figure out how to get back to the spaceport, Kori said, "Do you know what's going on?"

The other woman made a face. "Not from here, I take it?" Kori shook her head. "Picked a bad time to visit. I think the Empire finally caught on to our guest's presence." She had the same thick brogue that everyone on Gael seemed to have. She pointed up with a wink.

"You mean the Resistance ships?" The woman nodded. "You're okay with that? Your planet is okay with them?" She glanced over at the protestors. "Ah, never mind."

The other woman nodded. "Aye. Gael's got no interest in that langer of an Emperor. We were independent before and will be again!"

Kori's eyes went wide, fearing how others in the crowd would react, but noticed only smiles and nods. A few muttered agreements.

Jax walked up. "The next 52 we see. Get on it."

Kori nodded. The other woman moved back into the crowd.

Behind them, the sound of breaking glass caused most of the crowd to jump, then turn toward the massive shopping mecca. Jax and Kori wheeled in time to see several people dart inside the CostShaver through a broken pane in the glass entryway.

Jax looked at Kori. "It's been like three minutes, and they're looting already?"

She shrugged. "People gonna people." Several bus stop occupants were grumbling about the looters.

He rubbed his forehead. "They're not gonna deliver our order."

After Rudy paid the young man for his time, plus ample tip to ensure his discretion, Skip sealed up the *Osprey*. Rudy and Baxter were in the cargo hold organizing and reorganizing the few crates in the space when Skip beamed to them both: *Imperial ships have entered the system.*

Both droids stopped dead in their tracks.

Details? Baxter asked.

Nothing yet. The planetary network is all over the place right now. It looks like the Imperials are still a way out, the ship's SI replied.

What is the Goliath *doing?* Rudy asked.

Unknown. Too far for my sensors, and the feed from the spaceport network cut out. I have been attempting to hack back in, but I think they may have shut down the networking gear, Skip said.

Safe to assume they are not here because of us, right? Rudy asked.

Correct. Our entry records are under a different ident, Skip said, adding, *Once I was in the network, I also doctored our records to indicate that we arrived two days sooner, making it impossible for us to have come from Shise.*

Good idea, Baxter said.

Skip replied with a blushing emoji.

We should get ready to go, Rudy said. He made for the stairwell and the hollow center and its null gravity section. Reaching it, he shot up toward the bridge.

The sound of the boarding ramp deploying spun Baxter around toward the stairs that led down into the boarding chamber. *Skip?*

Do not worry. It is only the Himura family, Skip replied.

A moment later, Naomi and her parents stepped onto the cargo deck. Baxter came forward. "Good to see you all."

"Likewise, Mr. Robot," Hikaru replied, bowing.

Naomi stepped around her father. "Any word from Jax or Kori?"

From the ceiling speakers, Skip said, "I am afraid not. The local network is suffering from considerable interference. I have been unable to locate or connect with either of them."

"Wonderful."

Kana smiled. "Surely, they'll be okay. Jackson seems resourceful."

Naomi rolled her eyes. "He can be."

"Speaking of," Skip said, "I have him and Kori on camera. They should be here momentarily. I am beginning preflight checks."

Naomi turned to her parents. "You two should get situated upstairs."

Her mother's concern was obvious. "Are we in danger?"

Naomi grinned. "Usually."

"All spaceports have declared a ground stop," Skip informed. He continued, "Imperial ships have now settled into orbit over Gael."

"What about Commander Tight Pants' ships?" Jax asked.

Hikaru, Kana, and Kori all exchanged a look, the latter finally saying, "Excuse me."

Naomi released a deep sigh. "We kinda know the Resistance."

Kori's eyes grew wide. "I knew you gave them the Nemesis Fleet, but you never mentioned actually knowing them." She looked at Jax. "Certainly, no mention of knowing the tightness of anyone's pants."

Her friend sighed again. "We don't exactly advertise it."

"Because we're not part of it. We do the occasional job and cash the checks. Full stop," Jax insisted.

Skip said, "The Resistance ships appear to have pulled out of orbit but are still in the area."

Kori gave him a look. "Yeah, sure, sounds like it." She was all too familiar with Jax and Naomi's exploits regarding the Resistance. She also knew that it was an ongoing sore spot for her longtime friend and ex-boyfriend. Why he was still dead set against forming attachments to people was beyond her. Especially when he seemed to do it at random, anyway. He still fought it at every turn. She shrugged.

The group was spread around the common deck, trying to figure out their next move.

"Captain," Skip said. Everyone looked up at the ceiling. "I have managed to get access to a few planetary sensors."

"Okay. And?"

"I'm picking up a familiar IFF signal. It appeared a few minutes ago."

Jax clucked. "Well. Yeah, we've docked with *Goliath* a few times now."

Skip made his annoyed sound. "Not the *Goliath*. The *Buttercup*."

Kori's mouth fell open. "What?"

"You're sure?" Naomi asked.

Hikaru and Kana both said, "The...*Buttercup*?"

"Is that like a cruise liner?" Kana asked.

"Some sort of candy delivery freighter?" her husband asked.

"I cannot imagine a scenario where someone would be falsely squawking the *Buttercup*'s ident," the ship's SI replied.

"Okay, well, thanks." Jax said, putting the *Buttercup*

and its owners out of his mind. Then he looked around, noticing the look Kori and Naomi were giving him. "Uh, are you able to reach them? Hail them?"

The two nodded their approval of this decision.

"One moment."

Hikaru held up a hand. "Uh. Who or what is the *Buttercup?*"

Before Jax could reply, Kori jumped in with a grin. "Old classmates of ours. I'm sorta seeing one. Jax dated the other for a while."

Jax groaned. "They didn't need to know who dated who."

"Whom," Kana corrected, a sweet smile on her face.

Jax rolled his eyes. "They're..." He looked at Kori. "Friends." She smiled and inclined her head. He sighed. "Yeah, they're friends."

Naomi watched all this. "See, that wasn't so hard."

"Suck it," he shot back.

The overhead speakers chirped. "Jax? That you guys?" It was Marshall Delphino. His voice was shaky. There was static on the line.

Jax did his best to keep his face neutral. "Uh, yeah. Sure is, Marshmallow. How you doing?" He looked at Kori, who arched her eyebrows as she gave him an unblinking look. "Pal?" he added.

She smiled.

From likely over Marshall's shoulder, his younger brother Steve said, "We're a bit busy, Jax. What's up?"

Jax felt his cheeks burn. "Hey, Steve." He saw Naomi's parents mouth something to Kori, who nodded. The burn in his cheeks got hotter. "What're you doing here?"

There was a pause. "Here? What'd ya mean? Are you... Are you on Gael?"

"Sure are," Jax said. "Kori's here too."

"Hi Marshall. Hi Steve," she said loud enough to be picked up by the comm system.

"Babe? It's not safe for you to be here!" Marshall said, his voice strained.

"What's going on? Why are you two here?" Jax pressed.

"Why are *you* here? Wait. Are you working with the Resistance too? Were you aboard one of the other ships?" Steve asked. His voice was still a bit muffled, like he was behind Marshall.

Jax's eyes went wide. "You two are working with them? Doing what?"

"Hauling cargo. What're you doing for them?" Marshall replied. Static crackled through the connection.

Jax shook his head. "We're not. That's not why we're here. Are they bugging out? We heard Imperials arrived."

"No. They're not bugging out. They're slugging it out with the Imps. They told all of us contractors to clear the deck but, uh, we took too long and caught a stray missile. The *Buttercup* took damage to her wormhole generator. I had to put us down...Yo, Stevie, where are we?"

From somewhere not close to Marshall, his brother shouted, "Couple clicks outside Highgate! I think!"

Marshall came back. "So yeah, we're just outside Highgate. There's a clearing about a kilometer west of the city."

Kori sat forward, consulting her gPhone. She kept shaking her head and finally called Rudy over.

"So, you're stuck here?" Jax asked.

"Unless we can get some spare parts, yeah. The fighting was getting pretty heavy by the time we left the *Goliath*. Steve," he said his brother's name with as much venom as he could muster, "didn't want to take off before we finished unloading."

"They might need that stuff!" his brother protested from wherever he was aboard the brothers' ship.

"Cabbages will not change the outcome of the battle," Marshall shouted, clearly not for the first time.

Everyone aboard the *Osprey* exchanged a look. Jax gave a knowing nod.

Something outside and overhead exploded close enough to rattle the *Osprey*. Naomi looked at the ceiling. "Skip?"

"The fighting has descended from orbit. I am detecting several gunships and fighter class vessels duking it out over the city and the sea. One exploded a kilometer away," the SI answered.

Without asking Jax, Kori said, "Marsh, we can get you two off-planet."

Jax's head snapped around. "Excuse me, what?"

"You did say they were your friends," Kana Himura offered.

"We're not that close," Jax quipped, ignoring the look Kori gave him.

"Could you?" Marshall asked.

Jax gave Kori an icy stare before saying, "Sure. We can give you a lift off-planet."

Skip added his voice to the conversation. "Captain, I do not recommend lifting off unless we are planning to leave the planet. I am picking up more skirmishes overheard and stray blaster fire is filtering down as well. I suspect both will get worse. The spaceport is urging all ships to remain powered down and crews to seek shelter. If we lift off, it should be to depart the planet."

Jax nodded his understanding. "Can you get out of Highgate? I think they've got trains?" He looked around the lounge for confirmation but got only shrugs.

"Any chance you can get to us? We're kinda in the middle of nowhere and I'm not sure we'd make it. It's actually kinda hectic here."

Jax rolled his eyes before giving Kori another look.

Feeling bad for volunteering them, she said, "I can go get them. You all stay here and keep the *Osprey* safe." A distant explosion echoed through the hull.

Jax shook his head. "Our odds are better if we all go." He turned to Hikaru and Kana. "Not you two, sorry."

"If we had adventuring days, they would be long behind us," Kana said.

Jax smiled and turned to Baxter. "You keep them and the ship safe. As much as I'd like your firepower backing us up, if things are getting weird out there, a battle droid stomping around will only make things worse."

Baxter's optic sensor swooshed back and forth. He finally said, "Understood. I will ensure the Himuras and the ship remain safe."

"What about me?" Rudy asked.

"You are optional," Baxter quipped.

Naomi looked around the lounge. "So, how are we going to get there?"

"Highgate is 200 kilometers north-northwest," Skip offered. "There is a major highway for ground and hover vehicle traffic that connects it to Aberdeen directly." He added, "Marshall is correct. It appears that the planetary government has shut down the inter-city train system as several sections of maglev track have been damaged by the fighting."

Kori groaned. "That's only gonna get worse."

Jax slapped his palms on his knees. "Okay. Then let's get this show on the road."

After Naomi said her goodbyes to her parents, the three of them stepped off the *Osprey*'s boarding ramp. It rose as soon as they cleared it.

Jax looked around. "Time to steal a ride."

CHAPTER 9

Bringing up the rear, Kori said, "We could rent something." She pointed to the far side of the spaceport, where a ground vehicle rental agency was located. A large sign over the opening read, Big Jim's Rents.

"You paying?" Jax asked.

Kori sighed. "Sure. I did get us into this."

"Yeah, you did," Jax agreed.

She gave him a look, then led the way across the permacrete of the landing field. There were still dozens of ships parked around the field. Despite the chaos overhead, those few people they saw seemed to be going about their business as usual.

A corvette roared overhead, smoke billowing from a wound on its side. At the speed it was moving, it was impossible to tell who it belonged to. A pair of fighters roared by, hot on the corvette's tail, blasters screeching.

Naomi watched the ships rise into a cloud several kilometers distant. "This is weird."

"Come. The sooner we go rescue those buffoons, the better," Jax urged.

"Business as usual" seemed to apply in only a limited way. Big Jim's was closed.

"So, back to stealing," Jax said with a smirk. He looked at Naomi, then cocked his head toward a nice hover van parked nearby. Several vehicles were parked outside the agency while the nicer offerings were behind the wide and currently lowered transparent titanium security door. She frowned and moved toward the vehicle.

Jax turned to Kori. "So, like, this would make me square with the guys, right?" He made sure he was between Kori and the vehicle Naomi was kneeling next to.

She shook her head. "Try not to think of relationships as so transactional."

He made a face.

"We're in luck," Naomi said, standing. "Unlocked."

The hover van was emitting a low hum, the grav motors casting a faint glow under the vehicle.

"That's weird," Kori said, walking around the side of the vehicle. "They just left it unlocked and unsecured?"

Naomi nodded, smiling.

A loud commotion near one of the pedestrian archways into the spaceport caught the trio's attention.

"I have a bad feeling about this," Jax said as he climbed into the van.

Naomi took the passenger seat while Kori hopped in the back. "Dang, this is roomy," she said, patting the bench seat as she craned her neck to look at the bench seat behind her.

"You can window shop for your rug rat mobile later." Jax looked in the rearview display. "Remember how big Marshmallow's head is. Just saying." He pushed the throttle control forward, while guiding the van toward the spaceport's vehicle archway.

"You do know where you're going, right?" Naomi asked.

Jax guided the van around a corner following the wide tree lined street as it curved back and forth, switch-backing down the bluff. He held out his gPhone. "Rudy downloaded some offline maps for us." He handed her the phone. "Do not. I repeat, do not. Look in the photos app." He paused. "Or the HookupCentral app. Actually, don't—"

Cutting him off, Naomi said, "We get it."

From the backseat, Kori said, "Thirsty," shaking her head.

Naomi made a show of pinching Jax's phone between two fingers as if it were radioactive. She looked over her shoulder. "You want to navigate?"

Kori held up her hands. "I'm not touching that thing."

Jax clucked. "You touched that thing a lot."

She kicked his seat.

Despite the war raging in orbit and, more often than not, the atmosphere, there was still a fair bit of traffic. Gaels seemed to be largely nonplussed by what was going on. Jax couldn't discern any particular destination. Folks seemed to just be out and about.

"Distinct lack of panic," Naomi said as they passed a car with what looked like a family heading somewhere. Kori told her about their conversation at the bus stop. She shook her head. "They can't seriously think they can win this? The *Goliath* is powerful, but it can't hold this planet. Not forever."

"Tell that to the Gaels," Jax replied. "They seem to think they're the vanguard of a new Unification War."

As they reached the base of the bluff, another pair of fighters, these distinctly Imperial, was harassing a gunship. Despite its best efforts, it took a missile to its main drive and careened into a ten-story building that looked to Jax like a residential tower.

The trio made it out of Aberdeen with little trouble. With the help of Rudy's maps, they found their way to the G2 highway, which was sparsely populated with vehicles. Despite the fighting, the Gaels were largely going about their lives, more or less.

As they neared the edge of the city, a Resistance gunship crashed, sending debris in every direction. The crash sent a ripple of chaos through the surrounding area as several fighters roared overhead, first to ensure their target was destroyed, then others later to see if there were any survivors.

Jax wasn't sure if it was just his all-too-familiar run-ins with the Imperials of late, but the people of this colony seemed awfully blasé about warships fighting it out in orbit. The sound of ships overhead, especially exploding ones, was grating on his nerves more than he'd admit to the others.

The road out of Aberdeen was a smooth, chemically bonded duracrete, designed to last hundreds of years. The fact that less than half of all personal and commercial vehicles on the planet used wheels helped the roads last longer.

Kori leaned forward, poking her head between the two seats. "So...Commander Tight Pants, huh? Feels like there's more to that story." She wiggled both eyebrows.

Jax glanced to the side. He had hoped she'd let that go. "Not that much more. He just likes his pants a bit snugger than is appropriate for the leader of a Resistance group."

Kori turned to Naomi. "I thought we were friends."

Naomi smiled. "He's cute. Older, silver fox cute." She grinned. "I don't hate the pants."

"No pics?"

Jax made a face. "That's...that's not appropriate."

"Not of his crotch, you weirdo!" Kori protested. She looked at Naomi, mouthing, *Yes, his crotch.*

Naomi rolled her eyes.

Jax clucked. "Naomi's got her eyes on a different crotch."

Kori put a hand on his shoulder. "Oh, right." She grinned. "Coffee Guy." Kori and Naomi exchanged a knowing look. Coffee Guy was a topic Naomi had not held back on sharing. Kori said, "I'm aware of Coffee Guy's crotch." She made a face. "Okay, yeah, I think that's enough crotch talk." She leaned back in her seat. Jax nodded his approval.

They drove in awkward silence until a corvette from one side or the other roared by overhead. It loosed a pair of missiles at something they couldn't see before banking and burning hard, its engines screaming for more altitude.

"The Commander is out of his mind if he thinks they can pull this off," Jax said, guiding their van around a wrecked pair of cars. The occupants of both were nowhere to be seen. It was the first sign that anything was amiss on Gael, exploding spaceships not withstanding.

Kori nodded. "How many Nemesis ships did you give them, anyway?"

"Sold them," Jax corrected, then said, "Not enough to hold off the entire Imperial Navy."

Naomi nodded her agreement. "Last time we saw Clinton, he said they'd ambushed one of the big ones out around the New Melbourne sector. Maybe they've been doing better than we know? Picking off ships here and there?"

Kori's eyes widened. "How much do you two know?"

Jax sighed. "We haul cargo once in a while."

"You what?"

"Just cargo. Sometimes," Jax defended. "The money is good and we only do it once in a while."

Kori shook her head. "Really?" She turned to Jax. "You? Mr. I-Don't-Want-to-Get-Involved-or-Have-Friends?"

"I have friends!" Jax shouted.

"The droids don't count," Naomi and Kori said at the same time.

"Whatev—Oh crap." He jerked his head forward.

Traffic ahead of them was coming to a stop. A kilometer up the road, there appeared to be a barricade spanning both lanes of the highway, stopping traffic in both directions. Vehicles were stopping, pulling to the shoulder. Some even crossed the center of the highway, turning to head back to Aberdeen, not wanting anything to do with whatever this was.

The barricade looked like a hodgepodge of personal and potentially stolen civic vehicles. Several vehicles had been toppled and wedged against each other.

"That looks legit," Naomi said, rolling her eyes. "People lose their damn minds so quickly."

From the back seat, Kori said, "Can we go around?"

Jax watched the vehicles ahead of them. The barricade creators picked the perfect spot. This section of road dipped into a shallow valley in the surrounding jungle. Vehicles blocked what little shoulder existed. There was no way around, at least not in a vehicle. It was either back the way they came, or through.

"I don't think so," Jax answered.

Naomi opened her mouth, but Kori pointed out the front window. "Uh oh. Bridge trolls."

They were two vehicles from the hastily created barricade. A dozen armed men and women stepped out from behind the pair of large cargo hauling trucks that made up the barricade's "gate" to surround the delivery vehicle that was at the barricade.

Several rougher looking folks moved to take up positions along the top of the trucks, some even poking out from inside the vehicles that made up the barricade. Most of them were holding handguns or nonmilitary pulse rifles. They watched the men and women surround the van, then finally move away, the cargo haulers pulling away to create an opening in the barricade.

As the cargo van pulled through the opening, the car behind it accelerated, trying to push through the opening behind the cargo hauler. The crowd of would-be gate-keepers opened fire on the car.

"Oh, shit!" Jax and the two women said as one. The three of them watched as the car burst into flames. One occupant leaped out, engulfed in flames. After three steps, the body fell to the ground, unmoving.

Jax looked at the vehicle's dashboard. No other vehicles were behind them. "Fuck the Delphinos," he said, putting the vehicle in reverse.

"Too late," Naomi said, putting her hand on his, nodding out the front window. Some of the barricade creators were waving them forward, while others used a heavy roadwork vehicle to push the burning remains of the car off to the side of the road.

A burly, red-haired man in a kilt stepped out from the crowd of other kilt-wearing men and held up a hand for them to stop.

"See, not all dudes in kilts are hot," Jax said.

"Not the time," Naomi said.

Three more men separated from the group to surround the van, weapons held at the ready. The heavy cargo haulers pulled back together, closing off the highway. The wreck of the car that was ahead of them was still smoking. So was the body next to it.

The man Jax assumed was the leader reached the van. He tapped his pistol on the glass. Jax looked around. "How do you roll the windows down?"

Naomi shrugged. "Not my car." She looked past him out the window and made an exaggerated shrug.

The big man tapped the glass again. He looked less welcoming than he did a second ago.

"Christ, where are the damn controls?" Jax hissed.

While Kori was watching Jax, Naomi slipped one hand onto the center console. The bio-circuits in her hand pulsed as she explored the van's various controls. The window next to her started to drop, stopped, and rose.

Then the window next to Jax rolled down. He waved. "Hi."

"Where you heading?"

"Who's asking?" Jax eyed the man.

"The people with guns and a barricade, asshole. You an Imp sympathizer? Part of the Resistance?"

Jax put his arm on the edge of the window, trying to look casual. "Which one lets us pass?" His other hand fell to the butt of his pistol.

The burly, red-haired man harrumphed and raised his pistol. "Either woulda worked. It just changes the amount you pay."

Jax rolled his eyes. "Really, man? The Empire and Resistance are right up there slugging it out for the future of your planet, and you're shaking people down on the highway?" He made a show of looking around. "Guess cops are busy elsewhere." He glanced at the rearview display and noticed that several other vehicles had arrived, forming a line behind them.

Before the giant, kilt-wearing pirate could respond, Jax brought his blaster to bear and shot that man in the face.

Naomi screamed. "You blew his face off!"

"That's not cool, bro!" Kori shouted.

Jax reached down and threw the vehicle into drive. "It was set to stun!" he shouted, adding in a lower voice, "I'm pretty sure."

The large man's colleagues scrambled out of the van's way, firing wildly at the careening vehicle. Kori had her sidearm in hand as well, firing out the window next to her. "Fuck these guys. I'm not stunning!"

Naomi joined her, firing blindly at the would-be toll operators as plasma rounds burned into the vehicle.

Jax rammed into one of the cargo haulers' cabs, sending the driver, who had been waiting to move his vehicle to let them pass once they paid the toll, rattling around like a child's toy. Blaster bolts were striking the van, scorching the paint job and melting the decorative plastic bits and pieces. Jax had one arm out the window, firing blindly while trying to put the van in reverse.

Behind them, the line of cars and other vehicles waiting to pass broke into a wild dash, several darting into the gravel and scrub grass shoulder, others making frantic u-turns.

One of the barricade team got in a lucky shot, striking the van's right side grav lift. Something under the vehicle screeched before the back corner hit the duracrete, doing its best to gouge a groove in a material that was designed to resist starship engine thrust.

Jax put both hands on the control, handing his pistol to Naomi, who leaned out her window, firing both weapons at random. The van was getting harder and harder to control. He was trying to guide the wounded vehicle toward the shoulder when another blast struck the hood, sending a plume of smoke into the air.

The dashboard briefly flickered like a Christmas tree before going dark. Built-in emergency systems kicked in, lowering the van gently to the ground as the primary lift system shut down with a choked sounding rumble.

Blaster bolts were still striking the vehicle, but fewer than before. Jax took his weapon back from Naomi and fired several shots out his window. "These idiots aren't that smart," he said as a skinny man in a bright red and purple tartan patterned kilt fell to the ground, his chest a smoking ruin.

A blast struck near Kori, forcing her to duck away from her window and crouch next to the seat. "They're good enough shots!"

A flashy sports car shot past them, taking advantage of the chaos to continue on its way up the freeway.

Naomi slouched in her seat to avoid getting shot. "Where are the cops?"

Jax shrugged. "Eatin' donuts in a disaster shelter, probably." He leaned over Naomi's lap, sticking his arm out her window, snapping off a shot at a woman who was crouching out in the open, rifle in hand, spraying energy blasts across the van's body. She dropped to the permacrete with a thud.

Silence fell. Jax looked around. "Holy shit. We got 'em all?"

A family car sped by, kicking up gravel as it passed. It sideswiped the barricade but continued on. A pair of kids in the backseat waved as it passed.

Kori got off the floor and sat in her seat, looking around. "Huh. We did."

Several vehicles were gliding past the roadblock now, honking and waving thanks.

Jax consulted the dashboard, then looked at Naomi, who withdrew her hand discreetly, then shook her head. "Guess we're hitchhiking."

Jax sighed. "Yay."

"That's the second one," Hikaru Himura said. He was on the common deck staring at the bulkhead-mounted entertainment display. Skip was sending feeds from his various cameras to the large screen.

"Hopefully it fairs better than the first," Skip said from the ceiling. A large personnel transport was lifting off from the far side of the spaceport. A similar craft had launched thirty minutes prior, but a pair of starfighters had shot it down, forcing it to make a barely controlled landing outside the spaceport, crashing into the beach a half kilometer away.

"Fingers crossed," the elderly Asian man agreed. He turned to see his wife step out of the hatch leading to the ship's head. He raised an eyebrow.

She grinned. "I couldn't help myself. It was just so gross."

"It really was," Skip agreed from the overhead speakers.

Hikaru shook his head. "Okay, well now that you're done, want to help me in the computer bay?"

His wife dropped the elbow-length gloves she was peeling off. "What did you have in mind?"

"Yes. What *did* you have in mind?" Skip echoed.

Hikaru shrugged. "I don't really know, but, well, maybe we can offer some improvements. AI research is...was...kind of our thing." His face fell momentarily, remembering his and his wife's early career as artificial intelligence researchers, before being drafted by the would-be Emperor.

"Please be careful in there," Skip said.

On the display, the personnel transport was a fading dot in the clouds. It made it.

The pair reached the cargo deck and waved to Baxter as they made their way aft to the small computer and engineering space.

Baxter watched them pass, then wirelessly told Skip, *I am going to stand guard outside.*

Is that a good idea? the ship's managing intelligence asked, adding, *Droids aren't common or likely welcome here. You will stand out.*

I have my—

If you say cloak, I will blast you myself, Skip warned.

Baxter sent a frowning emoji. *I am nervous about the amount of activity at this port. Someone may decide to see if the Osprey is unlocked.*

Skip sent an eye roll emoji. *They would discover their error quite quickly.*

I am also bored, Baxter sent.

After a pause that, to SIs, was a lifetime, Skip sent, *Fair.*

CHAPTER 10

Jax and the women had watched dozens of vehicles pass the now unmanned roadblock, none even slowing enough to glance at them. After a few minutes, Kori shouted from the far side of the roadblock.

When Jax and Naomi came around the rear of the cargo hauler that would normally move to allow vehicles to pass once they paid the pirate's toll, they saw their friend standing in front of the most ridiculous and over-the-top hover car they'd ever seen.

"What the hell is that penis extension?" Jax asked.

The vehicle was almost as big as the van they'd stolen, but all the angles and preposterous accouterments made the actual interior space about a third smaller than their previous ride.

"Uh..." Naomi said.

"Oh, come on!" Kori held out both hands sideways like a game show hostess showcasing some prize. "A 4000 SUX Urban Assault model."

"Urban Assault?" Jax repeated, lowering his head to

stare up at her and the vehicle. "This has to be big man's ride," he added, pointing at the still unconscious red-haired ring leader he'd stunned in the face. He looked at the man, still senseless and spread eagle on the ground, kilt in an unfortunate position. "Definitely his."

Naomi nodded toward the tartan-kilted man. "Go get the fob."

Jax looked at the man, or rather, at the kilt that was covering more of the man's top half than bottom. "No."

"Don't be a wuss," Kori said.

"You do it, then." Jax jabbed a finger. "Do you see pockets?"

Naomi sighed. "This is ridiculous." She went to the car and placed a hand on the door. Her bio-circuits pulsed a few times, then the door popped open, rising on silent hydraulics like a wing.

Kori looked at her friend, then Jax, then back. "What? How did you open that?"

Naomi's mouth fell open. "Oh. Uh. Well, it turns out it was un—"

Kori shook her head. "Nooo." She squinted. "You just touched the door..." She cocked her head. "And it...Were there blue lights?"

Naomi turned to look at Jax before looking down at her feet, before looking back up at him.

He held his hands up. "Don't look at me!"

Kori watched this back and forth, then said, "Spill it!"

Naomi groaned. "I'll tell you on the road." She held out a hand to the car.

Jax rubbed his hands together. "This should be fun."

Naomi scowled at him as she climbed into the backseat, making room for Kori next to her.

Jax hopped up into the driver's seat. He looked around, then adjusted the seat once he found the control. "Off we go." He glanced in the rearview display. "Steve is gonna have to sit on Marshmallow's lap," he chuckled.

The 4000 SUX Urban Assault Edition's power plan thrummed, feeding power to the grav lifts evenly spaced along its undercarriage.

As the car rose a few inches off the ground, thick armor plates slid down, nearly touching the ground to make sure that anything the car approached would be shunted aside rather than driven over.

As they drove, Naomi told Kori all about her past, the Interface program, all of it. Jax added color and generally unhelpful commentary whenever he could.

Kori's identical Afro puffs bobbed as she nodded along to Naomi's story. At one point, she broke in, "So when you and Jax were on the train, checking the cars...that was..." She wiggled the fingers on one hand. Naomi nodded. "Wow."

"That's what I said," Jax agreed. He grinned. "Sorcery."

Naomi scowled at him. "Not sorcery. We've discussed this."

"And it works on anything?" Kori reached out to touch Naomi's hand only to have the other woman snatch it away.

"Anything with a computer in it," Naomi confirmed.

"So. Cool," Kori said, looking at her friend in a new light.

Naomi nodded. "If you could keep this on the down low, I'd really appreciate it." Her friend nodded. "Thanks." She turned to look out the window.

Unlike Aberdeen, Highgate wasn't a coastal paradise. Located nearly 200 kilometers inland, it was encircled by the planet's vast jungle, which dominated the non-coastal regions.

Between the sea and the lush jungle, the planet was a wealth of pharmaceutical raw materials, minerals, and more.

As the group rounded a bend, the squat glass towers of Highgate came into view. A damaged corvette roared overhead, followed by a trio of starfighters. The corvette banked, bringing its weapons to bear, firing wildly at the fighters. A lucky shot struck one fighter, sending it careening into the jungle, an oily plume of smoke rising into the sky.

"Odds they don't burn this entire planet down?" Jax asked.

Kori looked out the window at the smoke. "Not great."

Jax turned back to the road. "So, where are they again?" He snapped his fingers. "Never mind. I remember. Kilometer out." He tapped the navigation console, making a face. "Guess Urban Assault means offline maps." He nodded to the display. Highgate was near the top right of the screen, moving toward the center. On the left, a large open spot was visible.

Jax pointed. "Guess that's the spot."

From the backseat, Naomi said, "Looks like there's a service road."

Jax nodded, then slammed the brake as the vehicle in front of them came to a sudden halt. "Who'd have thought? Rush hour traffic in a war zone."

In the near distance, the smoke from the crashed fighter was already thinning.

The clearing they were looking for was in reality some

type of day camp. Tent pads lined the perimeter with fire pits scattered around. The center, which normally held a communal chow hall tent, currently held a squat cargo ship with scorch marks along her top and side, sitting crookedly atop the ruins of a wooden structure.

"Shit parking job," Kori said as Jax pulled into the large clearing to park next to the *Buttercup*.

The two Delphinos were standing next to their ship. Marshall waved as Jax pulled to a stop. He made an approving face. "Nice ride." His face was streaked with grease that had made its way to his long black hair, adding an oily sheen.

Jax and the two women hopped out. "You destroyed a campground. Well done," the former said.

Marshall pulled Kori into a bear hug.

Jax and Naomi approached Steve. "Thanks for the assist," he said.

Naomi nodded. "What're friends for?"

Steve nodded.

"I can't believe you two are hauling cargo for the Resistance," Jax said.

The younger Delphino shrugged. "The money's good. What can I say? Between our regular gigs and the occasional haul for them," he pointed up at the sky, "Marshall and I are finally doing pretty okay. Even got some long overdue upgrades for the *Buttercup*." He looked up at the ship. "For all the good they did."

Naomi put a hand on Jax's arm. "How'd you get hooked up with them?"

Steve's gaze shifted between them. "Are you guys...part of this?"

"What? No, don't be stupid." Jax made a show of looking around the destroyed campground. "That's silly."

Steve squinted at his friend. "You've been working with them!" He jabbed a finger into Jax's chest. "You took that gig and didn't tell us! Greedy asshole."

Jax shook his head. "It's not like that at all."

Naomi chimed in. "It's actually not. In this case, maybe this one and only case, he was trying to keep you two safe. Long story how we ended up involved, but we thought it would be dangerous to bring you in." She made a gesture to encompass the campground. "Case in point."

A loud rumble cut off whatever else was going to be said on the topic. A moment later, what looked like a corvette or maybe even a frigate—it was mostly engulfed in flames— roared overhead. Seconds later, an explosion shook the ground.

Steve looked in the direction the ship had been travel- ing. "That was close. We should see if they need help."

Jax shook his head. "We should do no such thing." He pointed in the direction the ship had gone. "You don't even know if that thing was Imperial or Resistance."

Marshall and Kori joined the conversation, the former saying, "If they're Imperials, we bug out. Easy."

"After we shoot 'em," Kori added.

"Easy would be heading back to Aberdeen right now," Jax replied, giving his ex-girlfriend a stern look, adding, "Shoot them?"

Naomi gave him a look. "If that ship was Resistance, it could have people we know onboard? Clinton?" She knew using the name of the man they'd helped find a new identity among the Resistance after he helped them piss off BioTek corporation would elicit a reaction from Jax.

"Fine!" Jax threw both hands in the air. "Let's go be heroes or some shit." He turned and headed for their borrowed 4000 SUX.

"They've been gone a rather long time now," Kana Himura said from the *Osprey*'s kitchenette.

Her husband was sitting at the small café-sized dining table bolted to the deck nearby. "I'm sure it's fine. Omi is a capable young woman. That Jax fellow seems to have a good head on his shoulders."

Baxter, standing near the staircase, said, "Your daughter is more than capable. She has saved Jackson numerous times. Mostly from himself, but also external threats."

"See," Hikaru said. He turned to Baxter. "How did they meet?"

"We met Naomi when we saved her and the relief organization camp she was working with from Imperial-backed rebels on Mariposa. She—"

Kana turned. "Mariposa? The world that's still embroiled in a civil war?" She was clutching the frying pan she was cooking okonomiyaki in. "The news said that the Emperor was considering quarantining the planet until the colonists either settled down or died off."

"Dear, careful. You'll burn your pancake," Hikaru offered, gesturing to the skillet in his wife's hand.

"Oh." She turned back to the cooktop, flipping the puffy souffle-like pancake.

Baxter continued, "At the time, she was just one more aide worker that needed to be removed from the planet. Later she showed up on Kelso station to proposition Jackson."

Hikaru turned his full attention to the droid. "Excuse me?" Fatherly pride deepened his voice.

Baxter made a rattling noise. "A business proposition." He paused, Hikaru giving him a look. Finally, the older man nodded. He continued. "Jackson resisted at first, but after stunning her and locking her in the smuggling compartment—"

"What now?" Kana asked, depositing an okonomiyaki onto a plate in front of Hikaru.

"She broke into his quarters." The eyes of the elderly couple widened. "Once we were underway to Themura with the crime boss, he—"

Hikaru held up a fork with fluffy yellow soufflé on it. "You know what? We don't need to know anything else." His wife nodded her agreement.

Wirelessly Rudy sent, *I am not sure who will be madder: Jax or Naomi.*

Baxter sent a shrugging emoji.

"Perhaps we should go help them?" Kana said. She looked at Rudy. "They're not far, right?"

Rudy bobbed on his smart material roller ball. "Correct. They are approximately two hundred kilometers away."

Skip cut in from the overhead speakers. "It is still too dangerous to fly. In the last thirty minutes, three flights of fighters have passed nearby—two of those flights were destroyed by other fighters or larger ships."

Baxter looked from one Himura to another. "I am inclined to agree with Skip. We can be most helpful to Jackson and the others by staying here, ready to assist them when called upon."

Rudy's squat cylindrical head spun in a full circle. Wirelessly, he beamed, *Do either of you think we should reach out to the Resistance? Jax and Naomi have a good relationship with them.*

Baxter shook his head. *No. At least not yet. We do not know what is going on in Highgate.*

I concur, Skip sent.

"Someone trade me," Marshall complained. He wriggled.

"Cut it out!" Steve said from under his brother. "Why are you on my lap? You're bigger than me." He shoved at his big brother, barely budging him.

"You shoulda thought about that before crashing," Jax said from the driver's seat. They were following another service road toward the greasy plume of smoke from the downed ship.

"Shut up!" the two Delphinos said as one.

Naomi spun around in her seat. "Don't make me pull this car over!"

"You're not driving," Steve groaned.

Kori sighed. "Like old times."

Marshall leaned over. "Want to trade? You can sit on my lap." He ran one hand through his hair.

She turned to him. "Been there, done that."

Jax smirked. "Yeah y—"

"No." Kori cut him off.

Naomi pointed off to the side. "Turn here."

Jax nodded, guiding their ride off the semi-maintained service road and down a narrow, not-at-all-maintained gravel track. Through the trees, he was just beginning to make out the orange of flames.

A few minutes later, they pulled to a stop. The flames and several pieces of the downed corvette were visible through the trees.

Jax looked at the group. "Better go on foot. If you spot a shock trooper, we bug the hell out." Nods all around.

The sound of shouting drifted through the trees. Marshall crept forward, ahead of the others.

"Marshall!" Jax hissed. The other man ignored him, coming to a stop behind a tree that gave him a view into the new clearing created by the corvette's crash. The wreckage spread out for nearly a kilometer. Pieces of metal and various other starship parts lay scattered everywhere, most still burning. While the bulk of the corvette was at the end of the kilometer-long gouge in the jungle, the survivors had gathered at the rear of the ship.

Marshall turned to look at the others. "Resistance," he whispered. He didn't wait for the others. He stepped into the crash site. "Hi!" he shouted, waving.

"Odds he gets us shot?" Jax said.

Everyone else shook their heads.

"Guys! Come on!" Marshall shouted from the crowd of men and women he'd met up with. He was waving frantically. "They need help!"

The others ran over. "What's wrong?" Kori asked.

One of the Resistance crewers said, "Three of our crew are trapped in the aft section!" She pointed at an opening in the hull that was spewing acrid smoke. "Main corridor crumpled."

"That looks bad," Jax agreed.

"Can you help?" she pleaded.

Marshall nodded. "Of course!" He looked at Jax and Steve. "Come on!" He didn't wait for them, heading into the ruined ship. Two uniformed Resistance crew members followed.

Jax sighed and followed with Steve Delphino on his heels. He stepped through the tear in the hull to find the interior of the crashed corvette dimly lit and full of smoke. It looked like one in five light strips was still functional, at best.

"Back here!" Marshall's voice called out.

Jax squinted. He tapped Steve's arm and pointed. He pulled his shirt up over his nose, gesturing for Steve to follow suit. They made their way to where Marshall and the two Resistance crew were at a pile of structural beams and other debris. On the other side, a heavy hatch jammed open an inch. They could hear voices from the other side. Frantic voices.

Marshall saw Jax and the others arrive and pointed to a thick beam that was wedged against the wall and the hatch's frame. "Help me out here!"

Jax joined him. The two strained against the beam.

From the other side of the heavy-duty hatch, someone shouted, "You can do this!"

Steve and one of the crewers joined in, taking positions just underneath the beam, putting their backs against it.

"On three!" Marshall shouted.

The four men pushed and pulled as one. The beam shifted. Then it shifted some more. Cheers erupted from the other side of the hatch.

"Watch out!" shouted one of the crewers behind the stuck hatch. The team moving the beam scrambled out of the way a moment before flames leaped out of the gap in the hatch.

"Christ!" Steve swore, brushing at his sleeve. He flapped his arm, batting at the flames. Jax helped him extinguish the flame.

From inside the other compartment, the flames faded. "You gotta hurry!" someone inside shouted. "The secondary exchanger's going critical!"

Marshall waved everyone back to the beam. "Come on, guys!" He got under the beam, bracing his back against it. Jax, Steve, and two other crewers each found a spot along the beam.

"One!" Marshall shouted. Jax adjusted his grip.

"Two!" Steve took a deep breath.

"Three!" Marshall shouted, immediately pushing with his legs.

The entire wreck shook, almost sending the group of men to the deck. The beam screeched as it slid across the bulkhead. With a final metal-against-metal groan, the thick structural support crashed to the deck. Cheers erupted from both sides of the heavy-duty hatch.

Something in the forward section of the corvette's remains exploded, shaking the entire structure. Someone screamed. Everyone turned to Jax.

"It wasn't me!" he defended.

Steve gave him a look. "Sure, man."

One of the crew members leaned down to a panel that the structural beam had blocked. "I think I can release the movement mechanism." He nodded to the panel he had opened. He shoved both arms into the opening.

"Hurry up, Abdallah!" one of the trapped crew shouted through the gap in the hatch.

The man turned. "Shut up, Pierre! I'm working as fast as I can!"

Jax and the Delphinos stepped back. Something else exploded. This time Jax couldn't tell which side of the hatch it was on. He turned to Steve. "Maybe we should wait outside?" Steve nodded and nudged his brother.

A few minutes later, ten men and women in smoke- and grime-covered Resistance uniforms came stumbling out of the wreckage.

"Is that everyone?" Jax turned to the source of the voice and blinked. Then blinked again.

The man, Abdallah, nodded. "Yes, sir."

"How many?" He looked around as he ran a hand through his dirty blond hair.

Abdallah frowned. "Three. Twenty if we count the walking wounded." He nodded toward a group of crew members sitting a hundred yards away on a piece of hull plating nursing various wounds. The big blond man swore.

The leader of the group looked around. Spotting Jax and the others, he came over. "Our thanks." They exchanged handshakes. He eyed the group, his gaze settling on Jax and Naomi. "I've seen you two before. Aboard the flagship."

Marshall raised a hand. "We've been on the ship too. Lots of times."

His brother rolled his eyes.

The other man ignored him. "The Commander speaks highly of you two. You're Jackson Caruso, Naomi Himura."

Jax ran a hand through his own soot-stained hair. "Yeah. That's us." He was pretty sure he was staring, but didn't much care.

"He's shorter than you imagined, right?" Marshall quipped.

That broke Jax from his ogling. He made a face. "Can we help you with something?"

"I'm Lieutenant Rogers. Michael Rogers."

Naomi smiled. "Nice to meet you. I recognize you as well. You're one of the Commander's right-hand folks."

Rogers inclined his head. "Been with the Resistance for a few years now."

Jax leaned in. "You've seen this dude before?"

She smirked. "Down boy."

He made a face.

"Sir, the mission," the man named Abdallah called out. He was clutching a data tablet in one hand.

Rogers nodded. He joined Abdallah, checking over whatever was on the tablet's screen.

"What mission?" Kori asked, turning to Marshall.

The bigger Delphino shrugged. "Beats me. We just ran cargo. Never left the hangar deck."

Steve nodded. "Yeah. No one mentioned anything to us, or any of the cargo ships, about any mission. They just said, get out of here. So, we got."

"After the cabbages were unloaded," Marshall added in a low voice. His brother glared at him.

Jax looked up as a pair of strike fighters roared overhead, another pair on their tails. One of the fighters launched a missile, the sound deafening to those below.

Naomi looked around the group. "This is so damn weird." She focused on Jax. "Did you ever get the impression they were in a position to go head-to-head?"

Jax shook his head. "I never really paid much attention."

She rolled her eyes.

Steven looked at Jax, then at Naomi. "To answer your question, no."

Marshall shook his head. "I dunno. Remember two trips ago? We were pretty sure we were hauling munitions, and there were a lot of ships coming and going."

Jax's mouth was hanging open. He composed himself. "Munitions?" He looked at Naomi.

"Musta been one of the jobs we turned down." She shrugged.

"Dodged that…well, bullet," Jax said.

Rogers walked back over to the group, his expression like he'd just swallowed a bug. "I need to ask for your help."

"With your mission?" Marshall asked.

Jax looked at him. "No, with picking his next vacation home." He shook his head.

Marshall punched Jax in the shoulder.

"Boys!" Kori growled.

Lieutenant Rogers and Abdallah watched, exchanging uneasy glances. The former cleared his throat. "The Empire has a research facility here on Gael. Actually, it was an Alliance facility first. Abandoned at the end of the war."

Naomi nodded. "That makes sense." She looked at Jax. "Those folks we met while shopping woulda lit this jungle on fire if they knew there was an Imperial facility here."

Jax nodded. "But how could the Empire hide something like that?"

Steve shrugged. "Most systems have at least moderate official Imperial traffic. A few shuttles here and there over years, diverting to this empty jungle…I could see it working."

Rogers released a growl. "If I may?" He was already tired of these bantering civilians.

Kori scowled at the men in her group. "Please." She turned to Rogers, smiling.

"The entire reason we're here is the facility. We learned about it six months ago. We've been planning this since then. Our intel is that," he nodded to Steve, "they slipped the resources in quietly over time once they found it. The Empire is patient."

Abdallah leaned in. "Sir, are you sure?"

Rogers nodded. "We don't have the manpower to continue the mission. We just lost nearly fifty people, all of whom were set to help the advance team penetrate the facility." He turned to Jax and the others. "If what the Commander says is true, they can help."

"Us?" Jax asked.

Rogers nodded. "He speaks highly of you two."

Marshall frowned. "Just them?"

His brother slammed his palm into his stomach.

Kori crossed her arms and sighed.

Jax cocked his head. "So, what's the mission? What's going on?"

Rogers looked up at the sky. "Lord help us." He looked at Jax. "I've been trying to explain this to you for what feels like the last year. The facility is a research lab. A big one. The Empire set up shop two or three years ago, we're not exactly sure when."

"Researching what?" Steve pressed. He was getting frustrated with his friends.

The Lieutenant inhaled. "We believe they're building a shock trooper droid."

"The fuck..." Jax drawled.

Naomi looked at him and nodded. "Yeah. That."

Marshall cocked his head. "But the Empire...the Emperor hates droids."

His brother was a bit quicker on the uptake and was aghast. He shook his head. "Imagine Baxter, wearing shock trooper armor."

The large Resistance lieutenant nodded. "He gets it." He added, "Our understanding was that the Alliance was looking into combat mechs that weren't as imposing as the Mark IXs. In fact, from what we learned from the *Goliath's* SI, the plan was for combat models that were human sized and shaped. Able to more easily blend in. Wear existing armor."

Kori whistled. "They'd be able to wear shock trooper armor..."

Rogers nodded. "Exactly."

Jax, his mouth hanging open, finally came back to himself. "If they have an unlimited supply of shock troopers...." He shook his head. "This is bad."

Naomi said, "Every independent station and colony, they'll have thousands of troopers on every one of them. There won't be a place the Resistance can hide. Hell, there won't be anyplace we can hide." She looked at Jax and the Delphinos.

Lieutenant Rogers nodded. He looked at each of them, then settled on Jax. "The lack of shock troops is the Emperor's biggest weakness. We need your help. Otherwise, there'll be no escaping the Empire."

"We can fit y'all in the *Osprey*," Jax said, nodding.

The other man pinched the bridge of his nose. "We're not leaving the planet."

"Ever?" Marshall asked. Everyone groaned.

Rogers squeezed his eyes shut. *The Commander must be out of his damn mind.* Opening them, he said, "The advanced team is at the research complex. We need to link up with them, go into the facility, and destroy it."

Steve made a face. "Why not just destroy it from orbit?"

"Shielded," Rogers said.

Abdallah, who had been watching the exchange all this time, added, "Plus, not exactly a great image for the cause: orbital bombardment of one of the few worlds that openly supports the Resistance." Rogers nodded his agreement.

"Of course." Steve groaned. He looked at Jax and the others. "So?"

Jax got a look on his face, turning to Naomi. "We're helping him, aren't we?" Steve and Naomi both nodded. Jax turned to the much taller and, in his opinion, far too handsome lieutenant. "We're in."

Rogers turned to Abdallah. "Stay here, take care of the others." The other Resistance fighter looked at Jax and the others, released an exasperated sigh, and nodded.

CHAPTER 11

As the ridiculously over-engineered but lacking-passenger-space grav-car eased onto the road, leaving the crash site behind, Jax said, "I'm too old for this shit."

From the pile of bodies in the backseat, Kori clucked, "You're 29. Calm down." She shoved an elbow into Marshall's face for leverage, which elicited a yelp. "Sorry. Happy to trade places with you, if you'd like."

He looked in the rearview, scowling. "How far?" He turned to Lieutenant Rogers, who was in the seat next to him because there was no way he would have fit in the backseat. As it was, the two women and the two Delphinos were jammed into the back. None of them looked comfortable.

Rogers consulted his gPhone. "Ten kilometers. There should be a service road on the right. It won't be marked." He had been tapping on the device since they got in the car.

"Ten clicks?" Jax asked, surprised they were so far from the target.

"We had a ground car in the ship's hold," Rogers said.

"Ah." Jax nodded. "Makes sense."

Naomi elbowed Steve as she leaned forward. "And the rest of your team? They're already there?"

Rogers nodded. "The advanced team has been planet-side for a month looking for the facility. We finally got the call about two weeks ago."

"Why didn't the advanced team take the place out?" Marshall asked.

"Not enough of them."

"Are there more of them than us?" Steve asked.

The big man shook his head. "Not sure. The Commander kept things compartmentalized. Even from me. My team was supposed to provide the muscle. There were fifty of us on the *Memphis*." His gPhone beeped.

"What is it?" Steve asked from the backseat, wriggling to get out from under Naomi.

Rogers looked at Jax. "Drive faster." He turned in his seat. "Command thinks the Empire knows why we're here."

"That's not good," Marshall offered.

"Uh, you're hard to miss. Massive old dreadnaught in orbit and all," Jax said.

"On the ground," Rogers growled, then added, "The Commander called in reinforcements to keep the Imperials busy but warns we might have company down here."

"Reinforcements?" Marshall asked.

Naomi leaned over, trying to keep Kori's hair out of her face. "Guessing the rest of the Nemesis fleet."

"Ohhh." Marshall nodded. "Right."

Kori looked at Naomi. "He's got other qualities."

Naomi smirked. "Must be big qualities."

Kori winked.

After turning off the road onto the service road, Jax pushed the vehicle's throttle control forward. The low whine of the grav engine rose in pitch. He shook his head.

Whatever this likely overpriced Urban Assault vehicle was supposed to be, it was under-powered, too heavy and worthless for cargo of any type. He looked in the rearview. He was enjoying the discomfort of his friends jammed into the back seat.

Rogers fidgeted in his seat. Even the front seats weren't spacious. Jax had no idea how the big red-haired man they borrowed the car from even got in the seat. "Two more clicks, then we ditch this ridiculous thing," Rogers said.

Jax nodded. "So, how long you been part of the Resistance?" He glanced to the side, but didn't turn his head.

In the back seat, Steve looked at Naomi. "Is he…"

She nodded. "Looks like."

Kori groaned. "And we have to watch."

Jax cleared his throat. "We can both hear you." His cheeks had taken on a crimson hue. So had Rogers', for that matter.

"Good," Kori said. She reached up to check on her two Afro puffs. Frowning, she felt like one was no longer the perfect sphere she'd styled it into.

The rest of the last two kilometers passed in silence. Jax watched the jungle pass by the windows. He had completely lost track of where they were. He was mostly sure that Highgate was somewhere to the west of them now. The canopy was so thick, even when the roar of a passing ship or fighter was audible, they couldn't see anything—the upside being that those ships couldn't see them either.

"I am not getting back into that thing," Kori hitched her thumb over her shoulder.

Lieutenant Rogers nodded his agreement.

"So, where're your friends?" Jax asked.

The big lieutenant looked around. "The last communique said we'd rendezvous northwest of the entry." He pursed his lips, then pointed. "This way."

Something or a few somethings roared overhead. As one, the group dropped into a crouch.

From somewhere up ahead of them, someone whistled. The group remained crouched, looking around. Naomi turned to the lieutenant, who was scanning the area ahead of them. He whistled a tune. Another tune came back in reply. He stood up, motioning for the others to follow.

Steve jogged up next to Jax. "You know I was really pissed at you, but now..." He gestured to take in the jungle, pointing at the burly Resistance man leading them. "Now, I'm not."

"Wait. Mad about what?" Jax asked.

Steve's eyes got wide. "Well, first you screwed us over on the whole Nemesis fleet thing. Then you didn't hook us up with the Resistance cargo deal you and Naomi obviously had going for quite some time."

Jax forced a smile. "I mean, we nearly died during the whole Nemesis fleet thing, like, more than once." He shrugged. "And, I dunno. This is feeling pretty death-y too." He paused. "Wait. You're in this one because of you, not me."

Steve waved a dismissive hand. Changing the subject, he asked, "What's it like working with them?" He nodded toward Rogers.

Jax shrugged. "I really couldn't tell ya, man. We don't socialize with 'em or anything." He made a gesture with one hand, flying it from one side to the other. "In and out."

"Really?" Steve scratched at his jaw, staring at his

friend. "Why? I mean, they're the Resistance. It's the freaking *Goliath*!" Jax could see Steve's excitement and did not share it. From Jax's point of view, his and Naomi's lives hadn't been better for having fallen in with the Resistance.

And the *Goliath* represented nothing more than the cause that took his parents from him. He shook the memory away. "I mean, the big tree in the middle is cool," Jax admitted.

"There's a tree in the middle?!" Steve threw both arms in the air. He turned to Jax. "Wait. The middle of what?"

"Are you two trying to get us killed?" Rogers called over his shoulder.

Rogers nodded.

Jax whispered. "The ship. There's a big tree." He made a face. "It is pretty cool."

A minute later, the group stopped. A man in dark green camouflage stepped out from around a tree. He looked at Rogers, then at Jax and the others. "B team?"

Rogers nodded.

"Excuse me." Kori dropped a hand to her hip.

Rogers shrugged. "Things are in the process of going sideways."

The other man nodded and motioned for the group to follow him. As they walked, he explained. "The facility is about a kilometer up ahead. We've scouted the perimeter and mapped the facility's layout."

Rogers nodded. "Troop strength?"

"Light. We think they meant to keep a low profile."

"Makes sense." Jax offered from behind the pair.

The advanced team man looked sideways at Rogers, then nodded to Jax. "Sure does."

"Well done," Naomi offered. Jax scowled.

The group stopped and the advanced team man said, "I'm Lieutenant Leo Chen." He gestured behind him. "My team is near what we believe to be the weakest section of the facility's outer wall." He made an effort to lock eyes with Jax and the others one at a time. "From here out, silence." He waited until he got a nod from everyone. "Let's go."

Jax looked around at his friends. It had been a while since he last saw Kori. She'd been busy with whatever she did on Jericho station and hadn't been back to Kelso since their adventure in the employ of the Crimson Orchid. He smiled. He'd meant to visit Jericho more than once and just never got around to it. It was always something that kept it from happening.

Jax looked at Marshall, then at Steve. The Delphinos he saw more frequently, but even after their adventures and the slight mending of their friendship, they kept themselves busy off-station. He sometimes thought about Steve and wondered if their brief relationship could have been more. A shake of his head: unlikely. He wasn't good at relationships and sort of valued having the Delphinos, at least Steve, as friends. Mostly.

Up ahead, the jungle thinned, and Jax could just make out the dull gray of permacrete.

Naomi sidled up next to him. "You know...Michael invited me to Terra Nova?"

Jax turned to her. "Like to live?"

"What? No. To visit. I said no because we were lying low. Now I'm gonna die on this ball of rock with you." She made a low purring noise. "That coffee."

Lieutenant Chen turned, skewering the pair with a look that made them blush.

Jax leered at her. "Coffee. Uh huh."

"This looks really prison-y," Marshall said, craning his neck. The top of the ten-foot tall permacrete wall shimmered. The energy shield wasn't visible this close to the wall, other than a slight ripple in the air at the top from the emitters strung all along the wall's top. From the center of the facility, floating nearly 200 feet above the facility, the shield dome concentrator glittered, acting as the focal point for the shield energy being emitted by the track along the top of the wall. The concentrator would float for as long as the shield was up, drawing power from the energy field. A small grav motor helped it get into position when activated.

Four more camouflaged Resistance personnel appeared from around the permacrete wall's curve.

Chen looked at the new arrivals, then Rogers, Jax, and the others. "My team."

Rogers pursed his lips. "So, you five, me, and these five." He shook his head. He'd faced tough assignments over the years, but this might well be the toughest.

In the distance, the whine of grav engines grew louder. A troop transport roared into view, approaching the facility. All of them scrambled back to the edge of the jungle and watched as the craft came to a hover several hundred meters away, along the wall's edge. The tracked shield emitters slid apart, opening a wedge in the shield all the way up to the top of the mast.

"Clever," Naomi whispered.

Once the facility's shield closed, the troop transport landing somewhere inside, Chen asked, "Okay—what's the plan?"

Rogers looked up from his gPhone, holding it so that Chen could see. "Reinforcements inbound."

The other man nodded. "Good."

Rogers took a deep breath, cracking his neck. "I think it makes the most sense for your team to run the distraction and coordinate with the new arrivals. I'll go with these five."

"What?" Jax asked.

Chen raised an eyebrow. "What space ace said. Care to explain?"

The big man nodded. "I think it makes sense for me," he nodded toward Jax and the others, "and them go in."

"Okay, still. Why?" Chen asked.

"You out of your damn mind?" Kori asked.

Rogers held up both hands, palms out. "Hear me out." Everyone remained staring at him. "Those two," pointing at Jax and Naomi, "secured the Nemesis Fleet for us." He nodded to them. "They also helped out on New Terra during that big storm."

Chen looked from Rogers to Jax and Naomi, eyebrows arched. "Really?"

Jax beamed.

"Interesting," Chen said.

"We helped, a little. With the fleet thing," Marshall grumbled. His brother elbowed him in the ribs.

The Lieutenant went on. "The Commander vouches for them. All four of them, really." He pointed to Kori. "Her, I don't know her, but she's spunky."

"Man, I'll spunky you," Kori said, her cheeks darkening a few shades. During the hike from the car to the facility, she'd reshaped her misshapen Afro puffs, and patted them for effect. Naomi looked at her, pointing to her hair, mouthing the word, *nice*.

Chen shook his head and pointed to his team. "And us?"

"You've scouted the exterior and know the lay of the land around the entire facility. You can keep the Imps running around out here better than we could. When the reinforcements arrive, you'll be even better off."

"If," Chen replied. "If the reinforcements arrive." He gestured toward the sky. "Lotta fighting going on up there, if you recall."

Lieutenant Rogers didn't need his colleague reminding him about the battles raging in air and orbit. In the distance, over the jungle's canopy, he could see the faint wisp of smoke from the remains of the corvette his assault team was aboard...where they'd be forever now.

Rogers inclined his head. "Fair. If reinforcements arrive." He spread his arms a bit. "Regardless, your team aren't infiltration specialists, and while that's not their forte, it is mine." He shrugged. "Unless you have a better idea?"

Chen frowned. "No." He turned to his team. "Let's get them set up."

The three men and one woman in Chen's group kneeled, dropping their backpacks. The woman—Jax saw Clarkson on her uniform—handed out power packs. "These should fit your blasters, but if not, we can swap out your weapon." Jax looked the power cell over, confirming that his blaster was indeed compatible with it.

"I'll need everyone's gPhone," one of the men said, holding out his hand.

"For what?" Jax asked.

"I'm going to set up a local area mesh between your

devices and ours. You'll have a channel for your team and an everyone channel."

Jax nodded and handed over his gPhone. While the man worked on their phones, Jax checked his pistol for probably the third time. He looked at Marshall, doing the same, and smirked. "Nervous?"

The bigger of the two Delphinos dropped his blaster to the ground.

Before Jax could mock him, a pair of transports roared overhead, flanked by four fighters. The fighters peeled off as the transports began to land a dozen degrees around the perimeter of the facility, nearly out of sight. They opened fire on something the group couldn't see as they rocketed away.

Rogers watched the ships pass. "Time to go!" He turned and accepted a satchel from Chen.

PART 3

CHAPTER 12

Besides setting up their mesh communication network, Chen's man had added as much map data as the team had collected while scouting the facility. It wasn't much, Chen admitted, but was better than nothing.

"This way," Rogers said. "According Chen's team, there's a support entrance a little further up. No guard, but they think upgraded security."

He didn't wait for any of them to reply, picking up his pace around the outer wall. Despite no one using the facility for nearly twenty years, the perimeter wall was surprisingly well maintained.

An explosion shook the ground. It felt like it was on the opposite side of the complex.

"How big is this place, anyway?" Steve asked as they reached a section of the wall that featured a protruding security entry. The airlock-like structure stuck out from the permacrete about five feet with a thick hatch at the end. It likely had a similar hatch on the inside where the lock met the wall.

The sound of weapons' fire filtered over to them.

Rogers moved to kneel next to the control panel for the outer hatch, when Kori cleared her throat. "Naomi is a whiz with electronics." When he looked at her, she shrugged. "She is."

Naomi groaned, rolling her eyes. "I can give it a try." Passing him, she turned to Kori, brows lowered into a glare. The other woman leaned back on her heels, grinning.

Naomi kneeled and said, "I, uh, need some space. You know...to do my thing." She made a shooing motion. "Need room for the hacking."

Jax ushered Rogers and the others away, the bigger man craning his neck to watch Naomi. Jax snapped his fingers. "Eyes forward."

Rogers looked at Jax, frowning. "She some kind of super hacker or som—"

"Here we go," Naomi said. She stood up as the outer hatch clicked and swung outward.

"Wow," Rogers said in a low voice.

"Damn, girl," Marshall said. He turned to Jax. "You two are in the wrong line of work, hauling cargo. You could make a killing as a heist crew." He rubbed his chin. "Like we did with the train!"

Jax rolled his eyes.

Naomi gave Marshall a flat look. "I'll go get the inner door open. Wait here."

"We should all go inside," Rogers argued. "In case one of their—"

"Wait. Here," Naomi said. She entered the service bay lock.

Jax stepped into the hatchway, facing out. "Genius needs space."

Rogers looked at Kori, who shrugged.

An assault shuttle roared overhead. It appeared over the

treetops a second after the sound of its engines warned of its arrival. The group ducked, taking cover in the shadow of the service entry. The ship slid overhead, its port and starboard antipersonnel weapons tracking back and forth looking for targets.

Just when the shuttle was angling to head back over the jungle, a pair of missiles streaked in, striking its shields. The shuttle returned fire, turning toward its attackers as two fighters—Jax thought they might have been the ones that escorted the Resistance shuttle down earlier—roared in, banking to split off to either side of their prey, their shields flashing from the shuttle's fire.

"Hurry up in there!" Rogers shouted.

The shuttle powered up its lift engines, rising to give chase to one of the fighters. The group waited, crouched next to the service entrance until they couldn't hear the shuttle or fighters.

Naomi popped her head out of the hatch. "We're good. Come on." She vanished back inside the small service passage without even waiting for the others.

The inside of the security passage was just a long tunnel through the facility's wall. At the other end was a thick door like the one they were all walking through. In the middle of the room was a solitary stool that looked like the last person to sit on it was with the Alliance military.

Jax wondered if his parents ever came to Gael. They left him on Kelso plenty of times in the months leading up to the war. Maybe they were part of this project?

The inner hatch opened into a vast dusty field that looked like the previous occupants of the facility had used as a soccer pitch.

Jax looked around. "Where to?"

Rogers took in the facility. Off to the left were four squat buildings that followed the curve of the wall; one was definitely a barracks, but the other three were nondescript and generic. To the right was a large three-story structure. Ahead and toward the center of the circular facility grounds was a building that resembled a flight control tower. Comm arrays and various other antennae stuck out of the structure's top.

There were also several much newer and Imperial-designed antiaircraft and surface-to-orbit weapons' platforms scattered around the property.

The big lieutenant pointed to the large building on the right. "Hacker girl, smaller Italian guy, and I. We'll take the right." He pointed to the others. "You go left."

"So, you don't know which building is the actual lab we're looking for?" Marshall pressed.

The big man leveled his glare at the older Delphino. "Sure, but I figured I'd have us waste time clearing other buildings first."

Jax raised his hand. "Can I change teams?"

"What about those?" Kori asked, pointing to the weapon platforms.

Rogers shook his head. "Getting into the facility is our priority. Presumably, whatever is down there has control of the weapons."

"Okay, cool. Whatever." Marshall turned. "Let's go."

Naomi watched Marshall, Jax, and Kori head off. She turned to Rogers. "Lead the way."

From inside the facility, the defensive shield that formed a dome overhead was nearly invisible, except for when an errant missile or blaster bolt struck it. At the dome's apex, the meter-wide collector hummed.

"It's weirdly quiet," Steve said as they walked through the soccer pitch. He pointed up. "The hum notwithstanding."

Rogers pointed at the shield. "Dampens sound." A transport passed overhead, raining blaster bolts on the translucent dome, each impact rippling. From their vantage point, the vessel's thrusters were silent.

"Eerie," the younger Delphino said.

They reached the building, stopping short a few meters from what seemed like the front entrance.

"The Alliance didn't believe in labels over doors?" Naomi asked. The building had been white once but was mostly naked permacrete and peeling paint flakes now. Several of the windows had yellowed, the transparent plastoid showing its age.

Rogers and Steve each shrugged, the former pushing the door open.

They walked in, looking around the empty entryway. Without looking over, Naomi asked, "So...Lieutenant Rogers...Seeing anyone?"

Steve turned to her, grinning. "Smooth."

Rogers pretended he hadn't heard the question. "This seems to be all offices."

Naomi couldn't feel any nearby computers, but that wasn't much of an indicator. She had trouble sensing computers and networks at a distance unless they were unshielded. Most weren't.

The trio explored the first few rooms, all nearly empty offices. "This must be an administrative building or something," Steve said. He reached over and poked at a damaged terminal on the desk before him.

"Don't touch that," Rogers snapped.

Steve's hand shot to his side. "It doesn't work."

"Doesn't matter. Just don't touch things."

"Man, I'm not a kid. I'm not gonna break things." He rested a hand on the terminal, which promptly tipped over and fell off the desk. Steve's eyes went wide as he looked from Rogers to Naomi and back. "Ghosts?"

Rogers rolled his eyes. "This is obviously not the lab we're looking for."

"Should we check the rest of this floor?" Naomi asked. She still hadn't sensed so much as a tickle of anything with data.

"I don't see the point unless you have a reason," Rogers said. Sweat plastered his hair to his forehead. He ran a hand through it, clearing his forehead and adding some semblance of control to his dirty blonde mop. It was warm in the ghost building. Warmer than it should be.

Naomi shook her head. "No, not really."

He turned to Steve. "That okay with you?" He gave the other man a look. "Unless you want to touch more things."

Steve nodded as his jaw clenched.

They reached the door as the sound of weapons' fire filled the air. Rogers stepped back, ushering the other two deeper into the building.

"That was inside the facility," Steve said. He turned to Rogers. "Your people?"

The big man nodded. "Assume so. They were gonna do their best to make it seem like they wanted to get through the main gate. Keep as many Imps as possible focused there." He gestured. "Okay, let's go." He tapped the earpiece tied to his gPhone. "Team 2, we're heading your way. Nothing in our building."

Things are getting more hectic outside, Skip beamed to the other two SIs aboard the ship.

Baxter, helping Kana Himura tidy up the common deck, sent back, *Should we lift off? Head to orbit?* He was holding the overstuffed chair in the air, while the older woman cleaned the deck beneath it.

Rudy was down in the cargo and engineering deck with Hikaru, working in the engineering space. He had both of this thin arms and tiny hands deep inside one of the secondary processing arrays that Skip used to manage the *Osprey.* He spun his squat cylindrical head to look at the older man. Wirelessly he sent, *I think we should keep the Himuras out of the loop for now. They are old. I do not want to cause them to worry. They might die.* He turned to Hikaru. "You are certain this will improve Skip's performance?"

The speaker in the ceiling made a coughing noise. "My performance is more than adequate already."

The older man nodded, looking at the ceiling. "Oh my, yes, Skip. You are quite good, much more than adequate." He held up a finger. "However, there is always room for improvement."

"Speak for yourself," Rudy said. He withdrew his arms. "I have completed my part."

Skip wirelessly transmitted, *We have not come to a consensus.*

Baxter lowered the chair. Turning to Kana, he said, "The common deck has never been this clean."

She bowed. "Thank you." Looking around, she said, "Tell me about Naomi's life. Is she happy?"

Baxter took in the room. *A little help.*

Rudy and Skip both beamed, *Not it.*

Baxter sent a string of frowning face emojis. He turned to look down at the small older woman. "I am not the best judge of human emotional states. But, yes, I believe she is happy. She and Jackson have forged what seems to be a strong working relationship."

Kana smiled. "That's good. We've been so worried."

Baxter tilted his head to the side. "If I may ask, why did you surrender her?"

The older woman put a hand to her chest. "We..." Her head fell, her eyes locked on the deck plating. "We didn't know what to do. The Emperor... well, Senator then, knew of our work with artificial intelligences, specifically sapient intelligences. His people approached us. They said they had a way for our family to support their efforts." She shuddered, taking a breath recalling the men in dark suits that had come to their door in the early days of the war.

She went on. "They made it clear we had no choice." She snuffled.

Baxter kneeled. "I am sorry if I have upset you."

Kana placed a hand on Baxter's matte black armored forearm, her pale wrinkled flesh standing out in contrast. "You've done nothing wrong. Hikaru and I made many mistakes in our lives: giving Naomi to those monsters, working for the Emperor." She closed her eyes. "I think I'll take a nap."

"Attention. Prepare for takeoff," Skip announced ship wide.

Kana looked up at Baxter. "What's going on?"

Baxter made to shrug when Skip announced, "The spaceport is getting too dangerous. Two Imperial troop transports landed twenty minutes ago. Imperial forces are going ship to ship. They have locked down three ships already. I have determined that taking off is now less risky than remaining here at the port."

Baxter looked at Kana. "Secure yourself in the lounge." Wirelessly he sent, *Rudy, bring Hikaru to the common deck.*

Copy that.

The sound of the *Osprey*'s grav-lift engines powering up rumbled through the deck.

Hikaru Himura came up the stairs and joined his wife on the large sofa, pulling restraints out from behind the cushions.

Rudy shot up through the center of the spiral staircase. Baxter looked at the two elders. "I will be in the cargo hold."

Outside the *Osprey*, a squad of shock troopers noticed the increasing whine of the engines. They raised their rifles as they fanned out around the ship.

Deploying antipersonnel weapons, Skip broadcast.

Outside the ship, near the wing roots, a pair of panels slid open. Blasters on articulated mounts dropped, swiveling to take aim on the Imperials.

The sound of weapons' fire filled the common deck. "Do not worry," Skip reassured from the overhead speakers.

The two elderly Himuras looked at each other, hands clasped together.

"I am a very good shot," the ship's intelligence said.

Marshall sneezed.

"Gesundheit," Kori said without turning. She was looking at a piece of equipment that had a crumbling yellowed plastoid housing.

"What does that mean, anyway?" the Delphino brother asked.

Kori turned. "What?"

"What you just said. Guh-zoon-tight."

Across the room, Jax rubbed his forehead, exhaling.

Kori shrugged. "I dunno, man. It's just what you say. Like since the beginning of time."

Marshall nodded, looking more thoughtful than Jax had ever seen him. "I doubt anyone knows what it means." His expression changed faster than any of them could track. He poked his head into a room. "Another science lab, I think."

"That makes five," Jax said. The trio had decided to work through the buildings in order. That plan had the benefit of putting the almost-certainly-a-barracks building last.

Jax did the same, poking his head inside a room that was enormous, easily enough space for a few hundred people to work. He looked back at the others. "This feels pretty lab-y. But doesn't look like many folks have been through here." He ran a finger over a deck. "In decades."

Kori came out of a door into the main hallway. "Yeah, thinking this ain't it."

Jax nodded.

Every room they had explored so far had been the same: dust and yellowing plastoid.

Their gPhones beeped, the earpieces in each of their ears crackled. "Team 2, we're heading your way."

Jax looked at Kori, then asked, "Why are we Team 2?"

"Because I said so," Rogers barked.

Jax rolled his eyes. "Whatever. We're in the first building. Almost done. Meet us at the next building." He tapped his earpiece.

"Uh, guys," Marshall called from somewhere at the

end of the hallway that ran the length of the building. He was leaning out of a doorway. He vanished back into the room.

Jax looked at Kori, who shrugged. The former said, "Maybe he found a cookie."

Kori shook her head. "Don't be mean." She winked. "Plus, he wouldn't share."

They found Marshall in a room at the end of the hall, passing a half dozen rooms that they hadn't explored yet.

"What're you doing back here?" Jax called. He noticed that this section of the building seemed to have less dust on the floor.

Kori entered the room Marshall was in first. "Woah."

Jax caught up to her. Marshall was standing in a room that mostly looked like all the others they had seen, except for two key things: It was clean, and at the back of the room, there was a reinforced hatch that looked like an elevator door.

In a low voice, Jax said, "What she said."

"Right?" Marshall said. He nodded to the hatch. "Locked down. I tried."

A door on the opposite wall swung in. "Skipping Indian next time," a naval officer said, stepping out of a small restroom, rubbing his hands together. He stopped short when he saw the three intruders.

The four of them stared at each other for several heartbeats before the naval man came to his senses, his hand reaching for the sidearm at his hip.

Kori beat him to the draw, sending a plasma bolt through his chest. The man's corpse fell back against the bathroom door, then slid to the floor. A charred and smoking hole sat in the center of his chest.

Jax turned to her. "What the actual hell?"

"What?" She shrugged. Jax pointed at the body. "He was reaching for his blaster. What was I supposed to do?"

"Stun him?" Marshall offered.

"Whatever," Kori said, sliding her gun back in its holster.

Jax gave her a look, then tapped his earpiece. "Team 1? Team 2. Think we found it...Yeah, the lab...Well, we found a heavy-duty elevator door... oh, and there was a guard." He looked at the others, making a face. "Yeah, a guard. Yeah, the first building on our side."

Marshall nudged the dead man's boot. When he saw the look the others were giving him, he said, "Just checking."

CHAPTER 13

"Well done," Rogers said, looking at the thick elevator doors. He turned to Naomi. "Think you can hack these?"

"Of course, she can," Kori boasted. When the big Resistance man and Delphino brothers turned to her, she coughed. "Well, I mean, based on getting us into the compound and stuff, you know, from earlier."

Steve rolled his eyes. Jax shook his head as he kneeled next to the access panel. He looked over his shoulder. "He have an access card?" he asked, nodding to the dead Imperial.

Rogers kneeled and started searching the body.

Steve did a slow circle, stopping in front of what they assumed was the entrance to the lab under the lab. "Why the hell did they hide it?"

Marshall looked over. "Hide what?"

"The lab." Steve gestured around the room. "This whole facility was Indie, right? Why hide a lab under their lab?"

Kori stared at him. "Good question."

Rogers stood holding a deformed piece of plastic.

"They hid the robotics facility under this base to protect the people here. The facility itself," he motioned around them, "was a public-private partnership with Gael and a handful of companies across the Alliance. They did all sorts of research and different projects. If I recall, the main thing they were up to before the war got heated was next generation grav plating and power cells." He shrugged. "If the scant records we found are correct, they built the lab facility down there because they needed new combat mechs and couldn't risk Senator Stenson's forces finding out. The Gaels were pro Indie, so it was a safe place to work."

"Think the mechs are still down there?" Marshall asked.

Rogers shrugged. "That we couldn't determine, but since we haven't already seen a flood of shock trooper droids throughout the Empire, I assume they had to start from scratch."

Naomi nodded. "Hope so. Maybe we'll get lucky and they're not even close yet."

"Jinx much?" Kori asked.

Naomi gave her a look.

Jax shook his head. "Droids dressed like shock troopers. I can't even."

Rogers waved the ruined security access card. "One way to find out." He looked at Naomi, eyebrows arched. "Think you can hack your way in without this?"

She looked around, sucking in a breath. She nodded. "Okay."

Jax moved to stand between Naomi and the others. "Okay, clear the—"

She held up a hand. "It's fine. Not like there's much room in here."

Jax and Kori exchanged a look, the latter asking, "You sure?" She looked around at Rogers and the Delphinos.

She nodded. "Yeah. It's getting exhausting." She smiled. "Besides, it's just him and Marshall."

Rogers looked from Jax to Naomi and back. "Excuse me?"

"What?" the big Delphino asked. He looked around at the others.

"Just watch," Naomi said, kneeling next to the security panel. She placed a hand on it and took a deep breath.

"What's going on?" Rogers asked.

Marshall nodded his agreement with the question.

"Tsk," Jax scolded.

Naomi's bio-circuits pulsed bright blue. She immediately sensed the various circuit pathways inside the panel. The blue pulses raced from her fingertips up her arm, vanishing into her rolled-up sleeve.

She turned to look at the others, blue pulses racing along the normally invisible pathways around her eyes and cheeks.

Lieutenant Rogers' mouth was hanging open. "What. The. Actual. Fu—"

"Almost there," Naomi said, cutting him off. She could feel the locking mechanism, the sensor that was waiting for the dead man's credentials, the multiple solenoids waiting to be activated. She closed her eyes again.

The panel under her hand beeped. The elevator doors slid apart. She looked up at the others. "Open, Sesame."

Marshall cocked his head to one side. "I thought it was says-a-me."

Steve turned. "Says-a-me? What, like great Uncle Mario?"

His brother nodded.

Rogers cleared his throat. "Is that really the biggest thing here?" He turned to look at Naomi.

Kori and Jax shared a look, then stepped into the lift. Rogers and Marshall remained where they were. Steve was patting his brother's shoulder.

Naomi stood and turned around. "Long story, short. Early Imperial program to counter independence espionage and intelligence droids. Wired young kids with bio-circuits and a few other tech gizmos." She rested a hand on her abdomen. "Trained us to infiltrate systems." She nodded over her shoulder. "Can we go?"

Marshall and Rogers nodded dumbly, following her into the lift. Marshall turned to Steve. "You knew?" His brother nodded. He punched him on the shoulder as hard as he could. "And you didn't tell me!?"

The *Osprey* shook as blaster bolts struck her shields, causing them to flare brilliant orange as energy rippled across them.

At the moment, Skip was dedicating almost all of his processing core to flying the ship. The Valerian Co-Op Infiltrator was not meant for dog fights; her few weapons were designed for space combat against larger enemies.

Luckily, between the three Sapient Intelligences aboard the ship, they had a moderately not-horrible plan. At least as far as Rudy was concerned.

Baxter, his feet magnetized to the deck, was standing in the center of the cargo hold, the large cargo door on each side open. Rudy, monitoring the sensor feeds, prompted him with which side to be on so that when an Imperial fighter came alongside, the big matte black combat droid was ready, his shoulder-mounted railguns sending high velocity slugs through the fighters, ripping them to shreds.

While Baxter handled their port and starboard defense, Skip used the antipersonnel blasters that normally were used to defend the ship when parked to harass any craft that tried to fly below them.

The two Himuras were clutching their shoulder straps as the ship rocked this way and that. The lights on the common deck dimmed and flickered as the power fluctuated, Skip redirecting power on the fly.

"This wasn't what I had in mind when we called Omi," Hikaru admitted. The deck jolted as his wife nodded her agreement.

Gunboat coming in from starboard, below us, Rudy sent to Skip.

A move he will regret, Skip beamed back.

Down in the cargo deck, a loud whine built in pitch.

Is that—? Baxter looked at the deck.

The particle cannon? Yes, Skip replied, adding a grinning emoji.

The Imperial gunboat roared toward the *Osprey,* coming in on an approach vector that would make it hard for Baxter to get a clean shot. The pilot, having watched the unknown ship knock almost a dozen fighters out of the sky, was trying an angle of attack he hoped would give him an advantage.

The copilot locked on to the ancient-looking ship. She looked over. "Target locked." Missiles in the ship's two missile pods were armed, their sensors locked in on the target. As her finger squeezed the trigger, a blinding purple light filled the cockpit, followed by the smell of ozone. Then nothing.

The particle beam stabbed through the gunboat,

burning through the cockpit into the interior weapons magazine. A nearly ultraviolet sheath of incinerated ozone haloed the beam. The beam continued through the ship into the ground, vaporizing everything within a quarter kilometer circle as it sliced through the ground.

Damn, Rudy sent.

Not out of the woods yet, Skip replied. He sent a dozen jet fighter emojis. *These are the closest to an Imperial fighter in the emoji library.*

A definite oversight, Baxter sent.

The *Osprey* tilted, roaring just above the thick jungle canopy as Skip increased their speed to put some distance between themselves and the oncoming Imperial fighters.

On the common deck, Kana looked up. "Mr. Ship. Is there anything you need from us?"

The speaker beeped. "I appreciate the offer, but you are safest where you are, and your being safe keeps me from having to waste processor cycles worrying about you."

Diplomatically said, Baxter sent over the wireless network.

The elevator trundled along for a minute before anyone spoke. Marshall was the one

to break the silence. "So...Can you, like, make things explode or move around?"

Naomi turned. "What? No. I can interface with computer systems and networks. Data. I can't control stuff." She shook her head.

"Well, kinda," Jax offered. Naomi glared at him. He

shrugged. "There was that time with the gliders." She gave him a dismissive look.

"Gliders?" Marshall's eyes were like saucers.

Naomi opened her mouth to explain, but the elevator jolting to a stop cut her off.

Rogers looked at Naomi. She scowled. "No, I didn't do that." She looked around the elevator car. It was blank. No buttons, no control panels of any kind. Not even a digital display of their progress or the floor. She looked at Jax, shrugging as she shook her head.

"Guess this is our stop," Kori said. She nodded to the door. "Marshall..." The big man returned a blank look. She sighed. "The doors. Please."

"Oh." He looked at Rogers. Both men moved to the doors, each taking a side. They pried their fingertips into the seam.

The others watched the two men strain against the elevator's inner doors.

"This always looks easier on action vids," Marshall grunted.

Steve and Jax watched, the former leaning over. "Should we help?"

Jax shrugged. "We're more beauty than brawn."

Kori looked at each and clucked, saying nothing.

The inner doors finally slid apart, revealing a floor in the middle of the doors.

Naomi kneeled to look at the lower floor. "The keycards must dictate what floor they go to." She pointed to the sides of the doors where control panels would be. "No controls in here."

"Let's go up," Rogers ordered. He pointed to the floor that was bisecting their view out of the elevator. There was more room above than below. "We can find the stairs."

"Why not just go down?" Steve asked.

"Someone stopped this car. They'll expect us to go down. This gives us time to get the lay of the land."

Everyone nodded their agreement with his assessment.

One by one, they climbed up and out of the elevator car. They were in a wide hallway, doors lining both sides.

"Damn. This place is big," Steve said as they gathered outside the elevator.

"So, where to?" Jax asked.

"How long can your forces keep the Imperials distracted?" Kori asked.

Jax looked at her. "Answer hers first."

The big lieutenant looked around the hallway, then at the ragtag group that surrounded him. He shook his head. "Not as long as I'd like. We don't have the resources to field the entire fleet. If Commander Roberts already brought in the reinforcement ships, that's all we've got."

Jax inhaled. "Then let's go be heroes." He started off down the hall, tripping over a piece of equipment someone left on the floor.

Even the big Resistance man couldn't help but chuckle.

Jax turned, glaring at the others without saying anything. He continued down the hall. He figured the stairs, if there were any, were at the other end of the hall-way, opposite the elevator.

"This level doesn't look used," Naomi said to no one in particular. "I wonder why?"

Rogers said, "If our intel is correct, there should be two, maybe three levels of lab and admin space. No idea if the Imperials are using it or not. Our intel is nearly twenty years old, and secondhand."

Up ahead, Jax turned, waving his arms at the others as he leaped into the nearest open doorway.

"Shit!" hissed Naomi. She knew Jax well enough to know that if he hid, she should hide. She gestured frantically to the others as she ran for the nearest doorway after grabbing Rogers' arm, pulling him with her.

Steve shoved his brother through the doorway opposite the one Naomi and Rogers went through, pulling Kori with him, just as the first shock trooper stepped in, weapon held out before them.

Seconds later, the door at the end of the hallway opened. Five shock troopers stepped out into the hallway, all with their plasma rifles at the ready. One of the troopers said, "Stupid rusty old door."

The lead trooper said, "The Commander said they stopped the lift between this floor and residential level." He pointed to the still open lift doors. "Chambers, go reset the lift."

"Copy that," a trooper said, breaking off from the group.

Steve leaned into the doorway to look across the hallway at Naomi and Rogers. He shrugged to them mouthing, *Now what?*

Rogers looked around. He and Naomi were in an unused conference room. He held up a finger to the two men opposite him. Looking around, he spied a terminal in the corner of the room, likely to control the room's systems. He nodded to Naomi, then the table. She inhaled, nodding. He turned to the door holding up a finger. *Wait one*, he mouthed.

Everyone moved out of view of the doors as the lone trooper reached the disabled elevator.

Naomi was pressed against the wall as much as possible, hand resting on the terminal. Her bio-circuits pulsed along her fingers and arm. She could sense the ancient code for controlling the lights and the holoprojector built into the table. She pushed deeper, hoping to find a network connection. Surely the Indies didn't sit in the corner to run meetings.

There it was! A connection to the greater lab complex. Her bio-circuits pulsed brighter.

"Any time now," Lieutenant Rogers hissed, making a hurry-up motion, his eyes glued to the light show racing up and down her arm.

Naomi glared, blue pulses of light flowing along her cheeks to encircle her eyes. This level had little in the way of usefulness, as far as she could tell. There were terminals in every room, but not a lot more. Wait. The lights. She reached through the network to the lighting controls in each room.

The trooper at the elevator turned as the lights in the rooms in the middle of the hallway flicked on and off. The four troopers at the other end noticed as well.

"It's working," Rogers whispered.

Jax looked around the room he'd jumped into. It looked like an office, some place an administrator would feel at home in. When the trooper walked past the door, he ducked under the desk. He pulled his pistol and checked the charge. He knew it was full, but it was reassuring to check. Not that pulse pistols did much against shock trooper armor —other than annoy the wearer.

He peeked up over the desk as the lights in the room opposite him flashed.

Not knowing the what others were up to, Jax watched two of the troopers walk into the room opposite his. Three other troopers walked by, one casting a casual look into the room Jax was in. He ducked under the desk before the trooper turned. He hoped.

"Check the room up there," one of the troopers ordered, then added, "Mavik, check that room."

Jax peeked up and over the desk again. He reached up and tapped his earpiece, whispering, "Two in the room opposite me. I'm gonna take 'em."

"Wait one," Rogers ordered. Jax was about to complain when the man continued. "Okay, on my count. Aim for their joints. The armor is thinnest there and pistols should be enough. Go!"

Jax checked the charge on his pistol again, then vaulted over the desk. It took four long strides to cross the room and the hallway into the office across the way. He had moments before he reached the two armored troops. He leaped into the air, throwing his body sideways into the back of the trooper on his right. As he collided with the startled trooper, he took aim on the other one, firing into the back of the man's knee, then turning his pistol to the man he was now riding to the ground. He shoved the muzzle of his gun into the trooper's neck armor and squeezed the trigger twice. Super charged plasma burned through the weaker material between helmet and torso armor. Other than the shout of surprise, the trooper didn't make another sound.

Jax rolled off the dead trooper as the second regained his composure. The trooper swung his rifle around. "You're dead, you fucking—"

Jax squeezed the trigger over and over, sending repeated shots of plasma into the trooper's helmet and neck. The trooper jerked with each impact until one of the charged plasma rounds found a soft spot in his armor.

As Jax ran across the hall, Rogers and Naomi were on

either side of the door to their conference room. The trooper that checked the elevator stepped in, his head turning to spy the big Resistance man. As he spun to raise his rifle, Naomi leaped on to his back, placing her palms on the sides of the trooper's helmet. By the time his plasma rifle was trained on Rogers, every component in the armor—including the power assist features—shut off, freezing the man in place. The man in the armor was now trapped, unable to move even a finger.

Rogers nodded. "Nice."

They could both hear the trooper screaming and shouting inside his armor. The pair spun at the sound of weapons fire. They stepped into the hallway as a trooper flew out of one room to slam against the opposite wall, their head at an awkward angle.

In the room the dead trooper came from, Kori was swinging a plasma rifle like a bat at the head of a trooper. The trooper was flailing their arms, trying to deflect the makeshift bludgeon.

Meanwhile, the Delphino brothers were wrestling with the remaining trooper. Steve was on the trooper's back, trying to pull their helmet off, while Marshall was trying to keep the hand with the trooper's pistol from taking aim at his brother.

In a flurry of movement, the trooper bucked Steve off, sending him skidding across the floor. Spinning, the trooper planted a foot in Marshall's torso, sending him across the room in the opposite direction.

Rogers rushed past Naomi, grabbing a piece of equipment she didn't recognize but that looked heavy. In a single fluid motion, the whatever-it-was went hurdling across the room to crash into the trooper a moment before their pistol lined up on Marshall, sending them to the ground in a tangle of armor and damaged office equipment.

Naomi watched Marshall get to his feet. He snatched the trooper's discarded pistol, sending several shots into the space between the upper torso and hip armor. The pistol clicked; the power cell drained. "Damn," she whispered.

Jax came in behind her. Seeing the carnage, he whistled. "Maybe they should replace these guys with droids." Five pairs of eyes turned on him. He stepped back. "Just sayin'."

CHAPTER 14

The stairwell was empty when Marshall pushed the door open. He went first, and she fell in behind him. "So, when we were hijacking that train on Themura, you weren't hacking anything?" Naomi shook her head, even though he was in front of her and couldn't see the gesture. He went on. "You were just doing your blue magic thing on each car?"

"Not magic, but yes," she said.

Marshall continued as if she hadn't spoken. "And when we were on the trail of the Nemesis fleet...you sabotaged the *Buttercup!*" This time, he did turn, looking over his shoulder.

She shrugged, pointing at Jax. "He made me."

Rogers cleared his throat. "So, are you, like, the only one with these powers?"

"Not powers," Naomi corrected, then she added, "No. There are a few of us left. Not many." She blew out a breath. "Scattered."

The big man nodded. "Interesting."

From the back of the small procession down the stairs, Jax said, "She won't hack banking systems. I asked."

The big man shook his head. "I wasn't going to ask." He turned to look at Jax. "You're shady."

Jax shrugged.

Marshall reached the bottom of the stairs. "Hey, do you get paid?"

"Who?" Kori asked. She looked at Steve, who shrugged.

Marshall clucked. "The Resistance. I mean, you all pay us." He looked up at Jax. "You too?"

Jax nodded.

"You get, like, a salary?"

Rogers stared at Marshall for a few seconds. "Open the door." The bigger Delphino gave him a look. "Please."

Marshall shrugged and pushed the door open slowly.

Rogers looked up the stairs at Naomi. "You know, the Resistance could use people with your...specific skills. The more the better."

She gave him a tight-lipped smile. "I'll mention it in the next newsletter." She made a go-on motion toward the now open door. He nodded and followed Marshall, Steve, and Jax into the hallway beyond.

Kori leaned in. "I get the impression you and Jax don't do as much work for these guys as the boys do."

Naomi looked over at her friend. "You know Jax better than I do." She waved a hand toward the men. "He's not a joiner. We haul cargo for them when need money. In and out as fast as we can."

Kori scoffed. "If you can believe it, this is nothing. He was so aloof as a kid." She smiled at the memory of secondary school on Kelso station. "And not cool-kid aloof. Sad-angry-kid aloof. Which didn't go far in the making friends area."

Naomi smiled. "Believable."

Jax leaned through the door. "You two coming?"

"Keep your pants on, hero," Kori replied. She made a show of patting her Afro. "Ladies are talking." He rolled his eyes. As they headed toward the exit, Kori leaned toward Naomi. "By the way. Loving your nails."

Naomi held a hand out, palm down. "Thanks. This color spoke to me."

Imperial blaster fire was pinning down Lieutenant Chen and his troops. Despite their best efforts to use their knowledge of the area surrounding the research facility, the Imperial shock troopers had surrounded them near the facility's main entrance. Chen was annoyed that a troop transport was coming and going with ease, depositing more and more troopers. Without air support, the Imperials were overrunning the area.

A few minutes earlier, the antiaircraft systems had activated the moment Chen and his people started their attack, keeping Resistance fighters at bay.

"Ojiwame! Take three and go west, see if you can push them back past that dry creek bed!" Chen shouted.

A woman in the same mottled camouflage as him nodded and tapped the shoulders of the three people nearest her, motioning for them to follow her.

The reinforcements promised by Rogers had arrived, but weren't enough. Those damned AA platforms destroyed the two escort fighters and damaged the troop shuttle, forcing it to make a crash landing. The shuttle's survivors rallied, but the combined force wasn't enough. They were taking fire from the Imperials protecting the facility's front gate, as well as a second group that had been dropped off after the Resistance shuttle crashed.

Another trooper crouch-walked over to Chen. "We're not gonna be able to hold out! Most everyone is down to one or two power cells."

The AA weapons barked repeatedly, sending Resistance fighters scrambling. Occasionally, the weapons would fire anti-orbit blasts at who knew what, but certainly not at Imperials.

Chen shook his head. "Rogers and those nobodies better fuckin' hurry up." He nodded to the other trooper, then stood, firing on the last spot he'd seen a shock trooper.

A loud roar caused Imperial and Resistance fighters alike to stop firing and look up, assuming another ship was coming in and about to get shredded by the facility's defenses.

The trooper next to Chen turned to him. "Are we expecting more reinforcements?" Chen shook his head. "Are *they*?"

Chen looked at the man. "How would I know that?"

A second later, a Valerian Co-Op Infiltrator roared overhead, two Imperial fighters on its tail. As the nearest AA weapons swung to open fire, a dark shape separated from the ship as it raced overhead. By the time the weapons opened fire, the ship was almost out of range, the two fighters still on its tail.

Chen held a hand up to shield his eyes from the sun to get a better look at whatever was falling toward them. "What the hell?"

As the dark object got closer to the ground, it shifted from a roughly spherical shape to that of a T.

"Sir?"

Chen waved a hand. The T continued toward the ground.

"That's a combat droid!" the man next to Chen shouted.

The droid tucked back into a ball as it hit the tree canopy.

A moment before he hit the ground, Baxter unfolded and extended his leg joints, allowing for greater give when he struck the ground, which he did with enough force to send a small shockwave in all directions.

Without waiting for the dust to settle, he stood, deploying both shoulder-mounted railguns and his forearm-mounted blasters.

He opened fire on the Imperial forces arrayed in a half-kilometer semicircle around the beleaguered Resistance fighters.

Chen saw the droid open fire and turned to his people, pressing his ear piece at the same time. "All forces, focus on the main gate." He spun, his free hand grabbing the man next to him. "Let's go. Push through!"

This is fun! Baxter transmitted. His sensors picked up three shock troopers moving around to his right, trying to come in behind him. He dropped to one knee, both arms held out in front of him, blasters barking, sending plasma bolts toward the troopers in front of him. Both shoulder-mounted railguns pivoted to point behind him, their telltale *zip-crack* announcing the deaths of the three would-be ambushers.

At least if you get hit, you won't fall out of the sky, Skip sent back. The *Osprey* twisted in a corkscrew as it rose. Every time the antipersonnel blasters in the wing roots came into range of the pursuing fighters, they opened fire.

Chen glanced over his shoulder. "Don't we have a bunch of those up on the *Goliath?*" He wondered why the Commander hadn't sent the mechanical warriors down. Then he wondered where this one random bot had come from. Why just one? He didn't think the Resistance had any infiltrators in the fleet.

The level below the dusty lab level was anything but dusty. Marshall stepped out into a wide hallway similar to the one above, except that it had plants and small chairs lining the entire length.

"Homey," he said, stepping aside to let the others exit the stairwell.

"This can't be the bottom," Rogers said, looking around. "This looks residential." He looked around. Most of the doors were closed, but there was an alcove about halfway down the hallway.

"Lift is there," Steve said, pointing to the pair of thick doors at the end of the hallway.

"Who the hell designed this place?" Kori wondered. She started down the hallway but made it only a few steps when the sound of a door opening reached them. She turned, both arms waving.

Everyone split off, pushing open doors, leaping into whatever was beyond.

Kori eased the door closed behind her and Steve. She turned to see him standing in the middle of a bunk room with beds for eight. "Cozy," she said.

Rogers and Jax found themselves in a supply closet. As

Jax eased the door shut, he heard voices. Maybe four people. He turned to find himself nearly nose to nose with the bigger man. He stifled a cough. "Intimate," Rogers grunted.

Marshall eased the door closed and looked around. "Naomi?" He was alone in another bunk room.

Naomi looked around the room she found herself in. "Well, well. Just my luck." Several processing cores in a rack at the back of the small room blinked at her. Through the door, she could hear voices getting louder. She darted to the back of the room, squeezing behind the various racks of processing cores.

Two lab techs and a naval ensign walked through the hallway. The darker skinned lab tech turned to her colleague. "Think they'll evac us?" She pointed to the ceiling.

The naval officer scoffed. "Nah. They'll mop the floor with those Resistance throw-backs. They'll never compromise this facility."

The other technician clucked. "Didn't you have to send a team of troopers upstairs just a bit ago because of a security alert?"

The first tech nodded. "And I heard they were about to breach the main gate."

The ensign shook his head. "Just a security patrol." He shrugged. "Besides, we've more troopers than we know what to do with." He grinned.

The trio chuckled as they continued down the hall toward the cafeteria.

"Anyone hear anything?" Jax asked over the mesh comm network. He wiggled, trying to turn around in the cramped space next to Rogers.

"Stop wiggling," the larger complained.

Jax glared. "Don't get any ideas."

"You wish."

"Do you two need some alone time?" Marshall asked over their earpieces. "I think I have some slow jams on my phone..."

Jax was about to reply when Kori said, "It's clear. I think there's a cafeteria or something at the other end near the elevator. They went that way. I think."

Jax turned to look at Rogers, a smirk on his face. The other man rolled his eyes and pushed Jax into the hallway. Marshall, Steve, and Kori came out of their respective rooms.

Kori looked around. "Where's Naomi?"

Steve looked around. "Third door on the right...I think. Maybe fourth," he said.

It didn't take long for the group to find the small server room.

Naomi looked up. Every bio-circuit on her arms and face was pulsing with blue light. "Get this. They call them shock droids."

"Shock droids?" Steve shook his head. "Not very original." His brother nodded. "I mean, 'storm trooper' sounds better."

Rogers shook his head. "That's silly. Shock bots..." He paused and shook his head. "Now they've got me doing it." He turned to Naomi, stepping closer to her. "Anything else?"

She nodded. "It's mostly just status reports, personnel stuff. But one of the researchers has been exchanging messages with someone on Nästa hem about the next phase of this project. Apparently, there's work being done there, too." She turned to Rogers. "Name ring a bell?"

He shook his head. "I mean, I know the planet. But that's it. Nothing in any records I've been privy to."

She shrugged. "Well, in addition to some seriously erotic correspondence, these two are looking forward to shipping the shock droids out to Nästa hem." She paused. "Or they're just eager to reenact some of their emails... Either way."

Jax leaned in. "You copied the saucy bits?" He leaned back when she glared at him.

Rogers was tapping his chin. "Okay. Then we gotta make sure this place is a pile of rubble. Whatever they're doing on Nästa hem, we can't let these droids get there."

Marshall snapped his fingers. "I knew that name sounded familiar!" He slapped an open palm on his brother's chest. "That ore job we did. Remember?" He looked around the group. "We hauled some ore to a factory on one of Nästa hem's moons."

"That's right!" Steve piped up. "They're known for making really strong alloys. Lots of shipyards use them for hull panels and stuff." His eyes went wide. "Didn't they make body armor?"

Marshall clucked. "Shit. Yeah. That saleswoman I was chatting up mentioned their armor line."

Kori rocked onto her hip. "Chatting up a saleswoman?"

Rogers held up both hands. "Nope. Not doing that." He pointed toward the door. "Let's go." He pointed to the center of the hallway. The door the trio of Imperials had just come out of sat closed.

Several million kilometers from Gael, a half dozen wormholes opened, ripping orange-purple holes in space-time. The INV-1217 *Hammer* and nearly a dozen corvettes and gunboats emerged, their shields immediately powering up, casting faint blue glows on their hulls.

Captain Lucy Scanlon watched as the task force's ships spread out around the *Hammer*. "Status report?" she called out.

Her executive officer stepped up next to her. "Task force in position." He looked over his shoulder at the tactical officer, who nodded. "Resistance ships ahead in orbit over Gael."

Scanlon nodded. "Arm all weapons. Target the giant monstrosity first." She nodded toward the *Goliath*, sitting in the distance surrounded by smaller ships. With the exception of the ancient dreadnaught, none of the other Resistance ships were a match for the Imperial force heading straight for them.

She turned away from the massive bridge window to look at the communications section. "Open hailing frequencies."

The senior comm officer looked at her junior officers, then turned to the captain and nodded.

Scanlon smiled. "Resistance forces in orbit over Gael, you have..." She turned to her XO, who held up both hands, fingers splayed. "...Ten minutes to surrender." She turned to the comm officer, making a slashing motion.

"Channel closed," the comm officer reported.

"Think they'll surrender?" her XO asked.

"I hope not," the captain said, a wicked smile on her face.

The *Hammer* was one of the most powerful warships in the Imperial Navy. She and her sister ships were the pride of the fleet. Destroying the Rebels' flagship would secure Scanlon's promotion to sector fleet commander.

Ahead of them, the *Goliath* and her small support task force moved, breaking orbit to head for the oncoming Imperial force.

Scanlon turned to her second in command. "Hope you're ready for a promotion."

CHAPTER 15

"Oh, shit," Kori whispered.

Looking over her head, Rogers grimaced. "Are they?"

"Turned off?" Jax said. "Looks like it."

"I fucking hope so," Rogers added.

Standing before them in neat rows were hundreds of droids. Each was roughly two meters tall, shaped like a human; hard points on their limbs and torsos waited for shock trooper armor to be attached.

"Are these...?"

"Shock droids? That's my guess," Rogers said. His shoulders slumped. "Hundreds of them."

Marshall made a face. "Thousands, I think."

Naomi nodded. "Yeah. They've been busy."

"And they look ready to go," Jax said.

The warehouse structure they were all standing in, with thousands of killer droids, was nearly a kilometer square. And it was full.

"Whoever designed this secret lab has problems," Steve said.

His brother nodded. "Seriously. Could they not just

have an elevator that goes straight down? Worst. Secret base. Ever." He held his fist out; Steve did the same, bumping his against his brother's.

Kori had moved off to look at the nearest shock droid. "So weird," she whispered to herself as she poked the blank faceplate. The droid had optic sensors where a human's eyes would be, but that was it for a face. Not even a vocalizer.

The droid was motionless and cold. They all were. Some type of standby mode.

She looked up and stopped. "Uh…guys?"

Naomi looked over to her friend, then followed her pointed finger to look at the massive warehouse's ceiling. "Huh."

Jax and Steve joined Naomi, following her gaze. The latter frowned. "I didn't notice any big ass doors when we were up there." He looked at Rogers. "You?"

The big man shook his head. "No." He checked his gPhone. Since they'd entered the underground complex, he'd had no signal. Holding the device up toward the massive cargo doors, he squinted. Still no signal. Hopefully Chen and his people were keeping the Imperials busy. He turned to the others. "Might be a faster way out."

Marshall knocked on the chest of a shock droid. "So… they're just… off?"

Naomi joined him, putting her hand on the droid's head. The bio-circuits pulsed along her fingers, racing up and down her arm. The lights faded. Her hand fell to her side.

"Blank." She moved to the next droid, placing her hand on its head. "Blank." She looked at the others. "I assume they all are."

"Maybe we still have a chance?" Jax said.

Rogers nodded to a huge door directly opposite the human-sized door they just came through. "Then we best get going."

As they crossed the large storage area, Steve whistled. "So many of them." The shock droids were lined up in groups of twenty, with a meter or two between them for technicians, and whatever else, to easily move around.

Kori came alongside him. "This is nuts. I'm not the only one that feels in over their head, right?"

He turned to her. "Just another day in Jax's orbit."

"One of these days, he's gonna get us killed."

"Probably."

They caught up to the others. Naomi was crouching next to the access panel set to the side of the massive doors. She had the hatch open and both hands resting on the circuit board inside.

Rogers loomed over her. "Everything okay?"

She looked up, blue pulses of light circling her eyes, traveling down her cheeks, eventually ending at her two outstretched hands. "The system's better designed than anything else we've seen. Lots of encryption. Top end."

"Can you—"

She scoffed. "Of course. Just gimme some space."

She turned back to the control panel. Every system was different. The Interface program's instructors had trained the kids on how to visualize different types of systems in order to better understand them.

Some of the kids hadn't taken to the idea as quickly as Naomi. Picturing computer systems in her mind had been second nature to her. This system looked like a massive temple. Getting through the front door was easy, barely took any effort.

Each floor of the temple was a maze of rooms and cross-connected corridors. On each floor, a staircase had a gate that she had to brute force her way through. Each floor's gate was better hidden and harder to get through to the stairs beyond.

The access controls for the door were on the top floor of the temple.

Some systems had ICE, Intrusion Countermeasure Electronics. Usually, simple programs or basic Rudimentary Intelligences. The trainers at the science division had used RIs to train the children. She could unravel one with ease after her first year.

In her mind, ICE were always defenders: ninjas, faceless droids, sometimes Smurfs, if the security felt particularly light. It was almost never a conscious decision, what form they took.

Oddly, this system didn't seem to have any ICE. Probably some weird prohibition of the Emperor's. He hated droids and nonhuman intelligences. *Idiot,* she thought as she reached what she assumed was the top floor of the temple.

In the real world, the heavy doors clicked, then separated down the middle, each side pulling away.

The group split into two bands, each taking a side of the large doors.

Jax peeked around the edge of the doorway. Dozens of people in lab coats were busy tending all kinds of pieces of machinery, none of which he could recognize.

Except one. He pointed to the far side of the room. "That's a big droid foundry," he whispered.

Rogers followed Jax's gesture. "Wow. Yeah. Bigger than those on the *Goliath*."

The gigantic machine was thrumming away, building one droid after another, depositing the blank frames on a hover cart.

Two technicians looked over at the heavy door, no doubt wondering why it opened. One of them said something to the other.

Marshall inclined his head toward the machine. "And running full tilt."

The massive automated device was whirring and clunking as it assembled the next shock droid, which looked nearly complete, missing only its arms.

Four of the blank units were standing on the hover cart near the machine, waiting for a final inspection before being moved to the storage warehouse.

Technicians busied themselves around the inert droids; diagnostic equipment plugged into ports under each unit's arm.

Rogers looked at the group. "We've got to destroy that foundry, every computer in there, and them." He pointed to the thousands of droids behind the group.

"Oh, is that all?" Steve quipped. His brother nodded his agreement to the sentiment.

"You volunteered," the big man replied.

"Did we, though?" Kori said.

Rogers shook his head. "Moot point now. We're here, and by the looks of things, they're gonna ship these things out soon. Since comms don't work, I can't tell Chen to call in an orbital strike." He shrugged. "So, it's time to hero up."

Jax pulled out his gPhone. "Well damn. I didn't even notice."

"The local mesh works so long as we're all within two to

three hundred meters of each other, but I noticed the loss of signal when we got off the elevator," Rogers said.

He leaned to look into the large work area beyond the door. There were fifteen shock troopers, including the squad commander, their maroon armor standing out against the gray of their underlings, all coming toward the massive door. They were less than a minute away from the team, likely wondering why the big doors had opened but no one had entered the lab space.

"I've got a plan," Rogers said.

"A plan?" Naomi repeated.

"A plan for twenty shock troopers?" Kori added.

"More of an idea, and there's only fifteen...Well, sixteen." He shrugged. He put a hand on Marshall and Steve's backs, shoving them into the open. Before they could react, he dropped the duffel bag he had been carrying on his back since they started and joined them, pistol held high. He released a mighty roar as he fired wildly into the lab space beyond, striking one of the shock troopers and a technician that was nearby. The trooper stumbled; the technician fell to the ground.

Not knowing what was happening, Marshall and Steve followed suit, screaming and opening fire. Two more shock troopers were hit, this time falling before the squad realized what was going on, dropping to their knees or behind work tables to return fire.

"Go!" Rogers shouted at the Delphinos as he stepped backward toward the inactive shock droids behind them. The brothers followed. He caught Jax's eye. "You know what to do!" He motioned Jax, Naomi, and Kori to step back from the door, pointing to the discarded duffel bag.

The trio turned and sprinted into the crowd of waiting droids. Fourteen shock troopers burst from the lab space, rifles held high and ready. They didn't spare a glance in any direction but forward, in hot pursuit of the intruders. Several took a chance, firing into the crowd of waiting droid frames. Jax, Kori, and Naomi flattened themselves as much as possible.

Jax nodded to the two women next to him. Grabbing the duffel bag, he ran around the door's edge into the lab.

On his heels, Naomi and Kori followed, the former darting over to the door's control panel. Having already cracked the system, it took less than a second to find the security protocols. The massive doors ground closed, locking under a code only she knew. Her bio-circuits barely pulsed.

When she turned around, she saw that Jax and Kori were standing with their weapons drawn. Dozens of lab coat wearing technicians were staring at them wide-eyed. Someone dropped a tablet on the floor with a clatter.

Rudy's head spun as the two elderly Himuras climbed the stairs. "You should be strapped in. It is unsafe to be moving around while we maneuver."

Hikaru darted for the pilot's chair, which was turned backwards, waiting for someone, usually Jax, to sit down. His wife made her way to the station Naomi typically occupied.

As the pilot's seat rotated into position, Skip said, "Please do not touch anything." The ship rocked as a missile impacted the shields. "Aft shields at sixty percent."

"That seems low," Hikaru said over the sound of alarms

going off. His gaze was roving over the console, familiarizing himself with it.

"Better than ten percent," Rudy replied.

Kana turned to the nav droid. "That isn't as helpful as you might think."

The *Osprey* roared over the jungle canopy, shaking trees and sending birds and other wildlife scattering.

One of the pursuing fighters flew through a startled flock of beings that looked like hairy seagulls, sucking several into its air-breathing atmospheric engines. The fighter rocked as the affected engine burst into flames. The wounded fighter trailed thick black smoke into the canopy until a fireball blossomed where it hit the ground.

"Well done!" Kana shouted, looking up from the sensor display.

"Thank you," Skip replied. "Though I have no control over the natural fauna."

"Take the compliment, Mr. Ship," Kana said.

"Three new targets inbound," Rudy announced. "Imperial. I believe they are heading for the facility." The tactical display in the main flight console updated for Hikaru's benefit.

"Aren't there supposed to be Resistance fighters around here?" Hikaru asked, looking up from the tactical sensor display.

"It does not look like very many of them remain," Rudy said. He added, "And none of them are within a hundred kilometers of our current location."

Once the Himuras joined Rudy on the bridge, the two SIs felt it would be rude to communicate wirelessly.

The ship rocked, the remaining fighter still firing on them. Skip flipped the ship over so that she was flying inverted. The two human occupants of the bridge screamed.

The inversion allowed the two antipersonnel blasters to open fire on the remaining fighter. Energy bolts from those blasters weren't powerful enough to cause the other ship any significant damage, meant as they were for people, not starfighters. The onslaught of energy blasts did keep its pilot busy, however.

Skip adjusted course, leading the trailing fighter right into the flight path of the three new arrivals. The twin blasters ceased fire as the Valerian Co-Op Infiltrator righted itself and banked to the right.

The pilot of the fighter on their tail had admirable reflexes, pulling his ship into a dive to avoid his colleagues. The fighter skimmed the treetops, sending birdlike creatures and debris high into the air behind it.

So close, Skip thought to himself.

As the fighter continued to struggle to gain altitude, it struck a tree that was thicker than the others, clipping its left wing, sending it into a flat spin that ended in a fireball rising up through the tree canopy.

Never mind, Skip added.

Back at the research facility, Chen was looking at Baxter, his mouth hanging open.

"I am Baxter." The articulated mount for his right shoulder railgun sparked and twitched where the powerful weapon had been torn clean off. The entire assembly for his left railgun was gone, leaving a jagged hole in his armored back.

"I'm Lieutenant Chen. Did Commander Roberts send you?"

"No. I am with Jackson Caruso."

Most of the shock troopers outside the research facility had been eliminated or had taken refuge in the complex's main entrance.

Chen shook his head. "I don't know who that is."

Baxter held one hand out level just under his shoulder. "About this tall with—"

Chen held up a hand. "Ah. Yeah, him. He and a bunch of other civvies went down into the lab with Rogers." He pointed behind him. "We haven't been able to push through their defenses, and we lost comms with Rogers' team pretty much right away." He pointed into the research campus. "We can't get more backup until those AA weapons are taken out."

Baxter turned his head toward the forest, his sensors pinging off multiple contacts. "They might be able to help." He pointed.

A dozen men and women riding on the backs of large, shaggy creatures that stood nearly three meters tall on six thick legs, emerged from the thick jungle.

One of the creatures came forward, its rider a burly man with a bald head and several types of weapons strapped to his back. He waved. "'Allo there."

Chen raised a hand. "Hi."

Baxter scanned the new arrivals. To a person, they each had at least two pulse rifles, numerous pistols, and several ground-to-air, shoulder-mounted missile launchers on them. He nodded to the leader. "Are you here to fight them?" He hitched a thumb over his shoulder toward the compound.

"Aye, lad. We are. Sorry we're late," the bald man

replied. He motioned to his colleagues, who nudged their six-legged steeds forward.

"Good," the big bot said. He turned and pointed to the compound and Imperial troops blocking the entrance. "We need to get in there."

The man broke into a wide grin. "Then what ya standing around for, metal fella?" He kicked the sides of his steed, urging the beast forward. He shouted something in a language neither Chen nor Baxter understood. His friends replied with hoots and hollers, following their leader.

Baxter watched the mounted Gaels charge toward the Imperial barricade and its nearly three dozen shock troops. "I will be right back."

As the combat droid moved toward the facility, following the creature-riding locals, Ojiwame, who had been standing silently nearby, leaned over to Chen. "Did you know we had local support? Or combat droids?"

Chen shook his head. "I'm as confused as you are." He smiled. "Glad I'm not an Imperial, though."

Ojiwame nodded her agreement.

The bridge of the *Goliath* rocked as another salvo of missiles made it past the mighty warship's point defenses.

"Status?" Commander Roberts called out.

His executive officer, currently standing near the rear of the large bridge, looking over the shoulder of one of the weapons control officers, stood. "Not great, sir! Shields are hovering around forty-eight percent with several sections offline. We've lost about thirty percent of our point defense battery coverage."

Roberts nodded and turned back to the expansive wrap-around window at the front of the bridge. Though the *Goliath* was meant to be crewed by droids, it had been built with humans in mind.

Five thousand kilometers away, barely visible, was the Imperial Adjudicator class warship *Hammer* and its swarm of support ships.

The two mighty ships and their smaller ancillary fleet had been slugging it out for what felt like hours but in fact had been just over one. Despite the *Goliath*'s firepower and size, the Resistance was losing. The loss of two light cruisers early on and had been a setback that the Resistance couldn't come back from.

Roberts' jaw hurt from clenching it, but he couldn't look away. He glanced toward the communications section. "Anything from our forces on the surface?" Rogers was one of his best people. If anyone could accomplish the mission down there, he could.

"I'm afraid not, sir," the young officer said, adding, "CAG reports our air strength is down to ten percent."

Roberts sighed. "Recall fighters. No sense in throwing away lives for no reason." The junior officer nodded. He turned to his flight team. "Prepare to break orbit. We'll fall back toward the second moon. See if the Imperials follow."

Lieutenant Commander Vale came to stand beside Roberts. "Thoughts?"

"We can't leave until we're sure Rogers destroys the facility."

"And Gael?" Vale asked, not taking her gaze off the distant Imperial force. An inset display layer on the transparent titanium had each enemy ship in brackets with tactical details displayed next to it.

"They knew we might not be able to hold." Roberts

hated the idea of abandoning the planet. The Emperor would surely punish the population for this.

Natalie Vale, his most trusted second, turned. "We're not beaten yet."

Mark Roberts, leader of the Resistance, nodded. "No, we're not."

"Sirs. The Imperials aren't pursuing," the lead sensor officer called out.

Roberts and Vale exchanged a look, then moved to join the sensor officer. On the display, the Resistance fleet, what was left of it, was moving from the planet Gael's orbit toward the second moon. The Imperial task force, however, wasn't following. The enemy was settling into orbit.

"We're less important than those droids. They need to ensure that they leave here with them."

"Good news for us," Vale offered. They were no longer in missile range.

"Bad news for Rogers and the other ground forces," Roberts replied.

"Mix in with the droids!" Rogers said over the mesh comm network. Out of the corner of his eye, he saw the two Delphinos split off from each other, darting in between clusters of inert combat droids.

The pursuing troopers were firing indiscriminately into the crowd of offline droids, sending them toppling into each other, smoldering holes blown in their torsos.

The three men scattered, firing over their shoulders at the pursuing Imperials.

Rogers spun, sending plasma rounds into a trooper that ducked out from behind a motionless droid.

"This is the last time we hang out with Jax!" Marshall huffed. He darted back toward the door they'd come through before. A blaster bolt shot over his head, forcing him to duck behind one of the droids. He looked up into the blank face of the thing and shuddered. Jax might like droids, but they unnerved Marshall. Especially when inactive.

"Maybe we should move off Kelso," Steve offered from a couple hundred meters away. He leaned around a droid, squeezing off a few shots. A trooper that was creeping toward him grunted before collapsing in a heap. "Got one!"

"Meet me by the hatch!" Rogers said. "We'll lure 'em up to the next level, get them further from Jax and the ladies."

Marshall looked around. "I'm there now." The torso of the droid he was behind exploded, sending him scrabbling toward another droid as molten bits of alloy rained down on him. He rolled on his back, finger squeezing his pistol's trigger. A shock trooper fell to the ground, knocking over a droid.

"Almost there!" Steve said. Marshall could hear him over his earpiece and out loud. He stood up and looked around. A blaster bolt struck the droid next to him. "Shit!" He ducked back down.

Rogers crept between rows of droids. The shock troopers had spread out, moving through the ranks of inert shock droids in search of the three intruders.

He could see the end of the warehouse. "I see you, Marshall. Be right there."

"Okay," the big Delphino replied.

Rogers crouched and sprinted the last few meters.

"There! By the door!" a loud voice boomed.

"Time to go!" Rogers said. He pulled Marshall up off the ground.

Steve bolted out from a row of droids twenty meters away. He was waving his arms.

A shock trooper stepped out from a row of droids, rifle held at the ready.

"Down!" Rogers shouted. Steve dove for the floor as the Resistance man raised two pistols, firing at the trooper. The Imperial's rifle spat supercharged plasma; one bolt struck Rogers in the shoulder. Grunting, he spun, falling to the world.

Marshall and Steve rushed to his side. "Did I get him?" he asked.

Marshall nodded vigorously. "You got him. Can you walk?"

The big man groaned, rolling to his uninjured side. "I think so." He held out his good arm. "Help me up." The trio ran for the door as more plasma rounds flew by them.

Pushing through the door back into the residential section, they collided with a pair of technicians. The two startled men screamed and stumbled out of the way.

"Stay down!" Rogers ordered as they rushed past. Steve slammed the hatch shut behind them, hoping to buy a few minutes. Pointing, Rogers said, "Stairs."

CHAPTER 16

The floor of the main complex was littered with equipment. The foundry at the far end was still emitting a constant low-grade rumble as it assembled droids.

The massive machine was being fed by an industrial fabricator, taking completed droid parts and assembling them. Every ten minutes or so, a blank droid frame would be lowered to the ground by a large manipulator and placed on the hover cart next to the one before it.

Jax smiled. "Hi, nerdy bad guys." He twitched his pistol. "If you could all step away from whatever the things next to you are, that'd be super."

"Who the hell are you?" a woman demanded, stepping toward Jax and the others. Her once jet-black, but now shot-through-with-gray hair was pulled back in a tight bun. She was holding a tablet in front of her like a weapon.

Jax opened his mouth, but Kori put a hand over it. "Who we are ain't important. We're here to shut all this down." She waved her free hand to take in the cavernous work space.

From inside one of the side rooms, a man in an impeccably tailored Imperial Navy uniform stepped forward holding a pulse rifle. "The hell you are! Die, Rebel scum!" He shouted, taking aim at Jax.

Kori shoved Naomi toward a workstation as Jax dove the opposite way. Kori fired blindly as she moved, causing several technicians to scream in pain and shock.

"Overreaction, my man!" she shouted.

"This is going well!" Naomi shouted from behind a work table as Kori dropped next to her.

Jax leaned around his own table, firing several shots toward the Imperial officer. "I dunno. This seems to be pretty par for the course." He withdrew and stood, taking shots from another angle and forcing the Imperial to dive behind a rolling cart, sending technicians scattering.

"I can't believe you people are making kill bots that will dress up like shock troopers," Jax shouted. "Irony, much?"

One of the techs popped his head over the workbench he was hiding behind. "They're not kill bots!"

Kori popped up. "Dude, what do you think they're gonna do with 'em? Use them as crossing guards?"

Naomi stood, fired twice, then ducked back down and crawled toward a bank of computer stations. Two technicians were cowering under the closest terminal. "Shoo!" Naomi hissed. The frightened pair stared at her wide-eyed. "Go! Now!" She urged, pointing her pistol at them.

Both technicians vacated the space in a mad scramble. Naomi looked up, noticing one of the terminals was still logged in.

She glanced over her shoulder. "Keep him busy!" She reached a hand up, feeling around the workstation.

Jax rolled his eyes. "Keep him busy, she says."

"I can hear you," Naomi replied over his earpiece.

"We all can," Rogers added. He sounded out of breath. "Can you three hurry the fuck up, please?"

Kori snickered.

Jax crawled closer to where the Imperial officer had been, shoving a crying lab tech out of the way. He looked at the man, younger than him. "You can't cry—you're building the means of oppression!" he hissed. Before the other man could reply, Jax popped up over the workbench. He squeezed off a few shots, scorching the wall.

At the rear of the large room, the foundry clunked and whirred; the thick manipulator arm lowered a newly completed droid to the waiting grav-cart.

"You Resistance assholes—just can't accept when you're beat!" the Imperial shouted. It sounded to Jax like he'd moved further back into the cavern, maybe back into the room he had come from. Jax could image a nicely appointed office full of awards and other Imperial nonsense.

"You Imperial turds are building shock trooper droids. Your boss hates droids!" Kori shouted, standing to add her own fire.

Jax stood and sprayed what might have been a small kitchenette with energized plasma. The coffee maker exploded. Somewhere, under one of the desks, someone was sobbing.

Naomi's hand found the edge of the processing core on the workstation. "Yes," she hissed. She crawled out from under the workstation enough to reach the device. "Here goes nothing."

She closed her eyes, concentrating on the computer under her hand. Her bio-circuits pulsed as she probed the outer edges of the system. The terminal was on the network.

She could probably reach every terminal in the entire lab complex.

Jax darted out from under the workbench he was crouching behind and sprinted across the room. Plasma rounds tracked behind him, turning workspaces into smoldering heaps and igniting several small fires.

He slid to a stop, returning fire. The Imperial officer ducked into the room near the back of the facility that he was using for shelter.

"Just surrender!" the man shouted from the room. "You'll be treated fairly."

"You surrender!" Jax shouted back, firing a plasma round into the room to help make his point. The blast splashed against the room's far wall, melting the framed picture it struck. He thought it might have been the Imperial officer shaking hands with the Emperor.

The Imperials at the gate saw the matte black combat droid sprinting toward them, followed by shouting and hooting locals riding six-legged creatures that looked like a cross between a horse, a bison, and a caterpillar.

"Fire!" the lead shock trooper shouted, raising his rifle. "Blow that damn thing apart!" He looked around. "And those other things, too!'

Without his railguns, Baxter's options were limited. There were too many troopers up ahead; his forearm blasters overheated when used too long. They were already in the yellow zone, according to his internal data stream.

Baxter. We are taking fire, Skip transmitted. Static

garbled the message. He ran a quick check on his internal communication suite. Signal strength was weak. The *Osprey* must be over ten kilometers away.

As he ran, panels on his forearms ratcheted open, allowing the blasters to slide back inside next to the reinforced actuators. As the blaster panels locked back into place, a separate set of panels opened, allowing the segments of a matching pair of chain blades to slide out. The moment the last segment deployed, the internal super strong metal cable pulled tight. The segments clicked into place one after the other, forming a razor-sharp, double-edged blade just over two feet long that protruded from beneath each of Baxter's wrists.

One of the Gaels caught up to him, nodding. "Nice blades, mate!" She spurred her mount forward. As she rode, she leveled her rifle and sprayed the Imperial line with supercharged plasma.

Baxter didn't have a mouth, but the sensation of a smile passed across his data sensorium. He focused back on his comm suite. *So am I. We are tied*, he sent back to Skip, adding, *Quite busy.*

Plasma rifle blasts lanced out. Baxter's optics homed in on each of the dozens of barrels pointed at him and his new friends. His tactical subroutines, currently overclocking at one hundred and fifty percent of normal, were predicting every trajectory.

Despite his imposing size, Baxter was far lighter on his feet than his large frame would indicate. He ducked and twisted, avoiding super charged plasma by mere inches. During his time aboard the *Goliath* in the massive ship's droid foundry, his internal systems had been upgraded to the latest specs, at least as far as the ship's database was concerned. Every actuator had been updated for increased locomotion response time. Carbon fiber muscle strands contracted and expanded as he moved.

He covered the distance in seconds, chain blades slashing through the two troopers nearest him.

One of the massive, six-legged beasts released a pained wail, stumbling into the dirt, its rider flying from his saddle.

Baxter helped the man up. *It is not a competition.*

We are inbound, Skip replied.

In the distance, one of the antiaircraft batteries opened fire on a passing Resistance fighter. Baxter didn't reply, but ran through several of the choicest expletives he'd picked up from Jax.

From their position, Chen and Ojiwame and a half dozen Resistance fighters watched the weird droid charge through the research facility's front gates and the two dozen entrenched shock troopers.

Chen turned. "They have blades?" His companion nodded. "If we survive this, I'm gonna have words with the Commander." He watched as the droid lunged to the left, blade sliding between the upper and lower torso armor hard points. "Let's go help him!"

Baxter spun in a low circle, taking the knee out from under another trooper, pulling his left arm back, his blade stained crimson. He snatched the dead trooper off the ground, hurling him at three others.

A trooper charged him, swinging a damaged rifle like a bat. Baxter parried a swing with his right arm. The sound of gun on titanium rang out. He pushed the weapon aside, swinging his other arm. A shock trooper helmet thudded to the ground. He kicked the body aside as two other troopers rushed at him, weapons barking as they sent high energy plasma his way.

Several plasma rounds slammed into him, scorching his

armored body. Internal systems were throwing alerts; several of his systems were becoming compromised.

The big bald man and his...whatever they were called... charged between Baxter and the closest Imperials, buying him a few seconds to redirect some of his repair systems. The man was bellowing a laugh that seemed out of place, given the situation. He had plasma rifles in each hand. Both weapons were firing nonstop.

The respite was short-lived. A plasma blast struck Baxter's knee, sending him toppling over. His internal system diagnostic flashed red. Two more rounds struck his left shoulder, reducing that arm's mobility by sixty percent.

Weapons' fire erupted behind Baxter. His sensors immediately identified the sound and energy signature as being different from the Imperial weapons. Bolts of plasma lanced over his head, striking several nearby Imperials.

Chen ran by, slowing a bit as he neared Baxter. "You coming, big bot?" He grinned and continued into the open courtyard toward the nearest antiaircraft battery.

"Why don't you just destroy the foundry and go? Leave us be!" one technician shouted from behind a large rack of processing cores. The devices must be spares: they were still wrapped in plastic.

"Don't you get it?" Jax asked. He nodded to the room the Imperial officer was still hiding in. "You're building them an army."

The Imperial officer leaned out and shouted, "An army to keep the peace!"

Kori raised her hand, firing at the door frame. "You shut up."

"We're building something new here. Something that will let the Empire ensure peace, everywhere, at once," the still hiding technician shouted.

"You mean subjugate everyone, everywhere," Kori replied, adding, "All at once."

While her friends argued with the facility staff, Naomi was busy sifting through the computers. Since the terminal was unlocked, she had free run of the entire facility's network. It was a treasure trove. Remembering what happened the last time she overloaded her internal storage mechanisms, she only copied what she felt were the most valuable pieces of information.

She was sifting through the research around these new droid frames when she sensed the internal communication network. With a thought, she piped the audio directly into her sensorium.

After listening for a moment, she swore. The troopers that Rogers and the Delphinos had lured away seemed to have the guys pinned on the lab floor two levels up.

She tapped her earpiece.

Kori looked at one of the braver lab techs. "What do you imagine is the outcome here?" She gestured to the massive machine behind them. "Thousands of droids out there waiting for shock trooper armor. They'll expand the Empire's reach to every corner of human space!" She took a breath. "The Empire's fist will close around all of us. Around everyone, everywhere."

A few more lab techs popped their heads up from cover, exchanging looks. The lab was looking like a prairie dog colony.

Jax noticed the uncertainty. "They'll be able to stomp

on every neck in the Empire at the same time. The slightest thing and these shock droids will be there. There won't be a street corner of the Empire that won't have a shock droid on it."

A pasty-skinned man cleared his throat. "Yeah. Bringing peace to every corner of the Empire." He pointed up at the ceiling. "Colonies like Gael, being antiempire, providing support for the Resistance...That'll stop."

Jax shook his head. "Peace through oppression? That's what you want?"

The droid foundry's huge manipulator lowered another inert droid frame onto the waiting hover cart. A siren blared, meant to alert the technicians to swap out the hover cart with an empty.

Jax looked at the office. "Look man. Come out, no rifle. It's over."

"Never!" the other man shouted back.

Kori sighed. "Oh, for crying out loud." She dove into the office, coming to her feet, pistol leveled at the man who was cowering against the wall next to the door. Her sudden arrival caught him off guard. "Drop it."

He growled, letting the rifle fall to the ground. She waved her pistol toward the door, and he exited the small office, scowling at Jax's grin.

Blaster fire peppered the wall, forcing Marshall to crouch as he ran through the stairwell door. "Shit!" he shouted, shoving his brother up the stairs ahead of him. "Why are we bringing up the rear?"

From several steps further up, Rogers shouted, "You're slower."

"You're slower," Marshall repeated, mocking the other man. As he rounded the landing, the door he just came through exploded inward, smoke rising from its melted face. Two shock troopers entered, rifles swinging to take aim up the staircase. Marshall slowed, leaning over to fire down on the two troopers, sending one to the ground and the other scrambling back through the ruined doorway.

He turned to see his brother a few steps ahead, waiting for him. "Go, dummy!" He started up the stairs as two more troopers entered, firing indiscriminately upward. Metal railings and duracrete melted under the barrage, showering them with red hot debris.

Rogers reached the landing for the lab level they'd come from originally. He shoved the door open. "Come on!"

The Delphinos followed him, slamming the stairwell door shut behind them.

"Now what?" Marshall demanded. "The elevator's probably still shut down." He nodded to the opposite end of the long hallway. The lift doors were closed. They had no way to know the location or status of the elevator car.

"We gotta thin those guys out," Rogers said. "We'll never get to the surface with them right on our tails."

Steve nodded. "And if we did, they'd just turn around and be Jax and Naomi's problem?"

"That's a bad thing?" Marshall asked.

"You two. There." Rogers pointed to an open doorway. "I'll take the other side. Let's cut these assholes down."

Both brothers nodded. They barely got into the dusty, unused lab space, turning back to the door, when the stairwell door at the end of the hallway burst inward, blown off its hinges.

Rogers leaned into the hallway, sending energized plasma into the smoking void of the stairwell. As the acrid smoke cleared, troopers darted out, taking a knee to provide cover while others came out behind them.

While it was a common joke around the Empire that shock troopers were more inept than not, ineptitude was the exception, not the rule. The first two groups of troopers peppered both doorways, slagging the frames and surrounding walls, while two more pairs exited the stairs.

Marshall looked across the hall to Rogers, who made a series of hand gestures. He nodded and turned to his brother.

"What's the plan?" Steve asked his brother.

Marshall shrugged. "Beats me. You go low, I'll go high."

Steve sighed. "Everyone says they want adventure. This is adventure, and no thanks." He looked at Marshall, crouched down. "Okay."

Both men inhaled, nodded, and leaned out just enough to peek down the hallway.

Rogers watched them and followed, leaning out to spray the hallway with supercharged plasma. The sound of several grunts told him they'd gotten a few troopers.

"Guys. Can you hear me?" Naomi asked over the shared mesh comm network.

"Bit busy," Steve said, ducking back just as a plasma round scorched the door frame behind him.

"Head for the elevator," Naomi said.

"It's closed," Rogers replied. He leaned out enough to peer the opposite way down the hall. The elevator doors slid apart. "Well, shit, you're handy." He looked across the hall. "I'll cover the two of you."

The two Delphinos nodded, taking deep breaths. Supercharged plasma was filling the hallway with smoke as blasts struck the doorways and walls. The smell of burnt plaster and electrical insulation had replaced the musty, old smell.

"This help?" Naomi asked a moment before the lights on the floor went out.

"Better than nothing! Go!" Rogers shouted. He stepped out into the hall and opened fire.

Marshall and Steve leaped into the hallway, making a dash for the waiting elevator. The pair got to the elevator and turned. "Rogers! Come on!" Both men dropped to a knee and opened fire from either side of the elevator car.

The sudden darkness threw the shock troopers into disarray. Several fell first to Rogers' fire, then the Delphinos'. Rogers dove into the empty elevator car, the two Delphinos covering him.

The lift doors slid closed as return fire scorched the car's back wall.

Baxter reached his left hand over to the mangled remains of his right-hand chain blade. Only half of the blade was still there. The other half had broken off inside the AA battery he and the Resistance fighters destroyed. With a twist and a tug, the damaged blade came free. The housing mechanism whirred as the rest of the blade slid back into his forearm.

Chen looked up at him. "You're super handy!" He nodded to Baxter's left arm. "Those just pop in and out?" Baxter nodded. "Neat. And you've got guns in there too?" Another nod. "And all the models like you—"

"Yes."

"So cool." He turned to the next nearest AA battery. "Okay. Ready for the next one?"

Baxter's right arm clicked and whirred. His blaster deployed, locking into place. He held his arm up for Chen to see. "Yup."

Chen shouted to his people. "Push through! We gotta secure the facility!" He pointed to an antiaircraft battery surrounded by shock troopers.

From the opposite side of the facility, skimming the trees, a pair of cargo shuttles, flanked by gunboats, roared in over the facility's far wall, through a wide wedge-shaped opening in the shield, near where Jax and the others had entered earlier. The gunboats opened fire on Baxter and the Resistance fighters, scattering them.

Baxter returned fire, but his forearm blasters just didn't have the power or range to do more than discolor the gunboats' paint jobs. He dove out of the way just in time as the nearest gunboat fired at him. Two Resistance fighters weren't as fast and met fiery ends as the high energy plasma that struck them vaporized their bodies.

Chen poked his head up. "This got worse."

Baxter nodded, raising both arms, firing at the nearest shuttle. His blaster fire had the same effect on the cargo shuttles as it did on the gunboats.

One of the gunboats pivoted in the air, sending blaster fire after the Resistance fighters.

"We have to fall back!" Chen shouted. "We can't take those gunboats!" He looked at Baxter. "Unless you've got missiles you haven't shown off."

"I am afraid not," Baxter said.

Chen watched their mounted friends thunder past, then turned to Baxter. "Only live once." He didn't wait for

Baxter. He broke into a run following the creature-mounted locals.

While the two cargo shuttles orbited the battle, the gunboats were making slow circles blasting the few remaining Resistance fighters they could find, raining death and destruction on the research compound.

The sound of screams and high energy plasma filled the research facility compound.

One of the antiaircraft batteries was unattended. Despite Chen's head start, Baxter got there first. The Gaels continued on, shouting, firing their weapons at anything that moved and looked Imperial.

Baxter looked over the AA battery.

Without Resistance starfighters to target, the device had gone into standby mode.

"Can you, I dunno, hack it or something?" Chen asked, crouched next to the massive weapon.

He turned to Chen. "No. But we are in luck." He pulled a panel aside, exposing the control interface. The interface was unlocked.

"I like you, droid."

"I get that a lot. I am quite likeable." Baxter turned to the controls, waking the powerful gun battery. He brought the pair of heavy plasma blasters online, swinging them toward the nearest of the gunboats.

The Imperial gunboat tilted, narrowly avoiding a shoulder-fired missile from one of the Gaels. It opened fire, sending plasma into the ground, blowing huge geysers of dirt into the air. Two of the Gaels and their mounts were hit. The screams were unpleasant.

Chen leaned over. "I think you need to activate the targeting system." He pointed. "This, here."

Baxter shook his head. "That will alert them they're being painted. I can target them myself." The big guns continued to swing around, lowering their barrels. "This should be fun."

The AA battery whirred briefly, its power plant coming to life now that it had a job to do. The nearest gunboat turned toward them after vaporizing another pair of Resistance fighters and a mounted Gael. Two of its wing-mounted blaster cannons swiveled toward the battery. Before the ship's weapons got anywhere near the droid and human, the antiaircraft battery's twin barrels barked, then barked again. The gunboat rocked with each impact of the powerful, charged plasma.

The gunboat's pilot tried to turn about, put some distance between her and the traitorous antiaircraft weapon blasting at her ship's shields, rocking the craft with each impact. The pilot, sensing her fate, brought the ship back toward the battery and accelerated.

"Uh oh." Baxter grabbed the back of Chen's shirt and darted away from the battery. The gunboat made it—barely —to the mobile weapon platform before its shields and armor failed. The explosion picked Baxter up off the ground, sending him flying.

"Are you sure this is a good idea?" Hikaru asked.

They'd evaded the last fighter long enough for Skip to knock it out of the sky with a glancing shot from his particle beam cannon. As powerful as the weapon was, it had a limited firing arc, a limitation that Jax complained about often.

"Sure? No," Skip replied. "But we can't stay airborne. I

have not picked up a single Resistance starfighter anywhere within several hundred kilometers in the last few minutes. I believe they have lost the sky."

"That is not good," Rudy said.

"I concur," Skip agreed. "Especially because I am currently tracking a dozen gunboats, troop transports, and what appear to be cargo shuttles, all squawking Imperial IDs."

"So, what? We land where Jackson and Naomi are?" Kana asked from Naomi's station.

"Unless anyone has a better idea," the *Osprey*'s managing intelligence replied. He opened the communications suite and sent, *Baxter, we are incoming.*

Not a good idea, Baxter sent back. *I have control of only one of the antiaircraft batteries. There are three—*The transmission cut off.

That is not good, Skip thought a second before his sensors detected a massive explosion followed by several targeting sensors sweeping the ship. "We are being targeted. Brace," he announced to the bridge.

"Wha?!" the two Himuras shouted in unison.

Baxter, you were supposed to secure the area ahead of us, Skip transmitted a split second before the *Osprey* tilted, her engines roaring as she banked and climbed. A series of blaster bolts lanced through the sky, several striking the shields.

As the ship pivoted, Kana said, "Are those people...?"

Her husband added, "Riding some kind of...well, I don't know what those are."

"They look like they're fighting with the Resistance, so who they are is not important at the moment," Skip said.

The *Osprey* rocked as another antiaircraft battery locked onto it and opened fire, followed by a third. Down on the ground, a group of the strange animal-riding humans was trying to attack one of the AA turrets, but it was defended by a ring of shock troopers.

Get us out of range, Rudy transmitted.

Excellent idea. I wish I had thought of that, Skip retorted. *All three batteries are —* The ship rocked, and something creaked like rending metal. *Locked on us.*

The small ship shook violently. The third battery was better maintained. It tracked the *Osprey* through every maneuver.

"Shields failing," Skip announced as the lights on the slight deck flickered. A pair of energy bolts punched through the cargo deck. A third bolt made it through and punctured the common deck, incinerating the lounge furniture and everything else in the space.

The two Himuras screamed. Smoke billowed up from the remains of the common deck. An alarm somewhere near the spiral staircase beeped twice, then the thick emergency seal slammed shut, cutting the bridge off from the deck below. Several displays flickered and went dark. Sparks erupted from junction boxes overhead.

"What's going on?" Kana Himura shouted. She was clutching the console in front of her. Her husband leaned forward to embrace his wife.

I am losing control. Skip beamed to Rudy. *I will crash as softly as possible.* Out loud, he said, "Please brace yourselves."

Rudy unclipped and moved beside the two humans. Deftly, his thin metal arms reached between the two, fastening Kana's restraints, synching the belts tight. "Hold on tight," he urged Hikaru.

"Brace, brace, brace," Skip said.

More bolts of energy ripped into the *Osprey*, ripping her

port wing off. Skip did his best to guide the ship toward the ground. More bolts slammed into the ship.

Metal panels slid up from the bottoms of the bridge windows, throwing the space into darkness as the ground rose to meet them, protecting the occupants as the ship plowed into the ground, sending a plume of soil and grass into the air amid the shriek of bending and tearing metal. The ship skidded, leaving a trench in her wake.

Baxter rolled himself over and sat up just as the *Osprey* crashed into the compound's lawn, throwing dirt and a few six-legged whatever-they-were in every direction. "That is not good." He consulted his internal systems. Several were flashing red, including his comm suite. After confirming that the damage was limited to specific systems, he rose. "Lieutenant Chen?" he called out.

Near the center of the large open compound, something rumbled. Baxter turned to see a one-hundred-meter-wide circle in the soil sink a meter before slowly turning clockwise, dragging clumps of grass and a few stray pieces of lawn furniture with it. When the circle reached ninety degrees rotation, it stopped.

"Chen?" Baxter called.

The remaining gunboat on the far side of the facility turned toward him. Baxter looked around one last time for his new friend. He was about to leave when he spotted a uniform half buried by debris.

Chen was unconscious. Baxter snatched him up and dashed toward a nearby building.

The gunship was picking off the Gaels and their steeds. Baxter saw the large bald man gesturing for his remaining warriors to fall back.

The circular depression stopped its rotation. A rumble

preceded a split forming right down the middle that grew and grew, the soil on top falling into the opening.

Baxter lowered Chen to the ground and peered around the edge of the building he was taking cover behind. He checked the status of his comm suite, still malfunctioning.

One of the cargo shuttles moved in, hovering over the massive new hole in the middle of the compound. The cargo module that made up the vessel's body lowered into the hole.

"Definitely not good," Baxter said.

CHAPTER 17

The ground rumbled. Jax looked around, his gaze settling on the lab coats he had finally corralled near a small break area off to the side of the cavern. "What was that?" He spared a glance toward where Naomi was still hunched over the computer terminal she'd been doing her thing at. "You okay over there?"

One technician clucked. "Us? That was definitely you. We're here."

Jax turned. "I've been here with you villains."

From his place sitting on the floor against the wall, the Imperial officer growled. "How are you not attacking him?" His glare was leveled at the group of technicians.

Jax raised his pistol. "Shut up, you!"

The ground trembled again.

"Uh, excuse me. I think that's the cargo door," a technician offered. She barely looked up to meet Jax's eyes before immediately looking at the floor again.

"The what now?"

Naomi's hands fell to her sides. "Yeah, it is. They're

taking the shock droids." She sounded wiped out. She was leaning heavily on the console beside her.

Turning to her, Jax made a face. "Who?"

The Imperial officer beamed. "We've won! Once those droids and the data on how to build them reach the Empire, every world will fall into line.!"

Jax ignored that man, moving to stand next to Naomi. "What's going on?"

She smiled. "We should go." Her hand, still on the console, pulsed briefly with blue light. The heavy security doors slid apart.

He nodded to the duffel bag he'd discarded in the middle of the floor. "We gotta blow this place up."

She nodded. "Taken care of." She cocked her head. "More or less." She turned to look past Jax to the technicians gathered in the corner. "You should go. Take your boss with you."

Jax stared. "What's going on?"

Kori joined them as the technicians fled into the larger warehouse space, their supervisor urging them on. "What's up?"

Naomi led them over to a terminal nearby, bringing up a security suite that showed several camera angles. One of them looked like it was from the roof of one of the buildings above. A huge circular opening loomed in the center of the compound.

Kori pointed to another feed. It was the warehouse on the other side of the massive doors a dozen feet away. On the screen, a pair of men were guiding dozens of the mindless droids into a cargo module. As far as she could tell, nearly a third of the warehouse was empty. "They're moving fast," she said.

The three of them leaned as far as they could to look into the warehouse area.

"They're taking them," he whispered.

Naomi nodded.

As the technicians reached the loading crew, the Imperial officer stopped, turned. "You Resistance scum," he shouted.

Naomi rested a palm on a terminal next to Jax. Every screen in the facility came to life, a five-minute countdown, counting down.

The Imperial looked from Jax and Naomi to the countdown. He scoffed and broke into a run, following the technicians and scientists out of the warehouse. Naomi watched him, middle finger held up.

Through the massive doors, Jax watched as the last of the technicians, urged on by their Imperial commander, pushed through the doors at the opposite end, making their way to the surface.

Naomi grabbed Rogers' duffel bag and ran toward the droid foundry, tossing the bag into the machinery and the half complete shock droid frame the foundry was working on.

She turned to Jax and Kori. "We should go. I'll explain on the run."

They nodded.

They reached the warehouse as another cargo module was filling; placid droids were marching into the module in orderly lines.

Kori turned to Naomi. "I thought they were empty?"

Naomi shook her head. "Beats me. Must have some minor RI to move them around or something. I know their processing cores are intact and online, but..." She shrugged again.

"How do you know—" Jax started, but stopped when Naomi waved a hand.

"No time." She pointed toward the doors and the stairs they'd come down earlier, beyond them. "Four minutes."

"Let's roll!' Kori said, not waiting for the other two, heading for the doors.

Marshall burst through the door of the building into the waning sunlight as one of the cargo shuttles roared up and out of sight. The shield dome was no longer active. "The fuck is that?"

Steve pushed past him. "I'm more concerned with that." He pointed to the wide-open hole in the ground, a newly arrived cargo shuttle hovering over it.

"Christ," Rogers swore. "They're taking the shock droids." The cargo shuttle was lowering its cargo module into the hole in the ground.

"Oh, shit," Steve murmured.

Marshall and Rogers turned to look at Steve. The younger Delphino raised his arm, pointing. The other two men followed his gesture.

"Oh," Marshall said, his voice barely a whisper.

Rogers turned back to Steve. "What am I looking at? That piece of shit crashed over there?"

"Not the gunboat," Steve replied.

Rogers made a face. "Ah, that other piece of shit? So?"

"That piece of shit crashed over there is our ride," Steve replied, his face ashen. "It normally looks better."

"No, it doesn't," Marshall said, scoffing. "That thing's always been a piece of crap."

Rogers nodded toward the *Osprey*. "Let's check on it." He pointed off to the edge of the facility's lawn. "We can go around that side. Stay low, avoid that gunboat."

Said gunboat was slowly orbiting the cargo shuttle hovering in the center of the lawn over the massive hole full of shock droids.

The three men made their way around the building, keeping to the edge of the facility's lawn.

"Who was aboard?" Rogers asked as they moved from one building to the next. They passed one of the remaining antiaircraft batteries, silently scanning the sky for a target.

"Oh, shit!" Steve said.

"What?" his brother asked, then smacked his forehead. "Oh, God. Her parents."

"Whose parents?" Rogers looked from one Delphino to the other. They'd stopped walking.

"Naomi's," Steve whispered.

"She brought her parents to a war zone?"

Marshall shook his head. "Sorta. Well, not really. They came to get us. The *Buttercup* took damage when we left the *Goliath*. We had to put her down," he motioned in the general direction he thought the ship was in, "over there a ways."

Steve pointed elsewhere. "The *Buttercup* is over there."

"Whatever."

They stopped talking as the whine of the hovering cargo shuttle grew in pitch. It was leaving, its cargo module fully retracted back into the ship.

Rogers put a hand on both men's shoulders. "Let's get to your ship, see what's up. Maybe we can make contact with Chen and his people."

"If any of them are still alive," Marshall said. Rogers turned to glare at him. "Sorry."

With the shuttles coming and going and the surviving gunboat nearby, things had gotten quiet. They hadn't seen any shock troopers, or sadly, any Resistance troops anywhere in the facility's green space.

They rounded a corner and came face to face with a matte black combat droid. Mostly matte black, at least. Dirt and clumps of grass clung to its joints and several damaged sections of its armored body. A brownish gray liquid oozed from several places.

Baxter stared at the three men, who stared back slack-jawed. "Hello." His voice was scratchier than usual. His vocalizer was damaged.

Rogers leaned over to look behind the large droid. "Chen?"

Baxter looked over his shoulder. "He is injured." He stepped aside. "My sensors are damaged. I am unable to ascertain his —." Whatever he said at the end was lost to static.

Rogers kneeled next to his colleague, checking his vitals. He released a breath and turned to the others. "He's alive. His pulse is weak, but there. He needs a med bay."

Steve moved to the far end of the building they were next to. "The *Osprey*, or what's left of her. If the med bay is intact..."

Marshall nodded to Chen. "Let's get him to the ship."

Baxter turned. "Off we—." Static. He scooped up the unconscious Chen and headed off.

Jax pushed open the doors, stepping out into the evening light and immediately stumbling back into the building.

Kori and Naomi stared at him. He looked up. "Gunboat right outside."

"See the others?" Kori asked.

"Or shock troopers?" Naomi added.

Jax closed his eyes, trying to replay what he'd briefly seen. He shrugged. "No idea. So bright."

The two women groaned.

Kori pushed past him to ease the doors open. "Uh, Jax…"

"Yeah?" He joined her at the door. She pointed across the facility's lawn. On the opposite side of the massive cargo access tunnel, with a cargo shuttle hovering over it, was the *Osprey*. Or what was left of it.

"That's…That's…" Suddenly his brain wasn't processing properly.

Naomi came up behind them, peering over Jax's shoulder. Her hand flew to her mouth. "Oh, Jax." Then her face contorted with realization. "My parents."

Jax's mouth closed.

Kori slid past them. "Okay, let's go." She pointed to the left. "We can work our way around that way." Her two friends nodded silently.

She turned to Naomi. "They're fine, your parents."

She turned Jax around to face her. "Skip and the bots are fine."

Jax didn't reply.

As they eased around the edge of the building, the cargo shuttle in the center of the facility pulled its cargo module up, securing it into the fuselage.

Naomi slowed, watching first the gunboat, then the shuttle rise into the evening sky. "Guess that was the last of them."

Kori and Jax slowed to watch the two ships vanish into

the sky. The former shook her head. "This was a fun failure."

The ground shook, and from the center of the facility a thick plume of smoke began to billow.

Kori smiled. "Okay, not a total failure."

When they reached the *Osprey*, Jax saw how bad the damage was and his heart sank. He'd never seen the *Osprey* in a shape this bad before. The port wing was completely gone, the remains of the common deck visible through the hole where the wing had been. Flames danced up through several of the many holes in the hull.

The intact starboard wing had carved a 30-foot-long gouge into the ground before catching and sending the ship's nose into the topsoil. Everywhere Jax looked, dirt and debris had been thrown in all directions.

Naomi rushed to the ship. The boarding ramp was crumpled in and half buried. "That's not going to open," she said.

Jax joined her. "Skip!" he shouted. "Skip! Blow the boarding ramp!"

No answer. That was worrying.

Kori walked around from the ship's rear. "Guys! Come over here!"

"What?" Jax shouted.

"I said, come over here! Not shout back at me!"

He sighed and headed aft, Naomi in tow.

Kori was standing next to the starboard side cargo door. It was ripped half off its track, not open but more importantly, not closed. "Tada." Kori made a sweeping gesture as she bowed.

Naomi stepped toward the damaged cargo door. "Help me open it more." She grabbed the door's edge, grunting as she tugged on it. Jax and Kori joined her, pulling and pushing, doing nothing to budge the heavy door.

"Mom! Dad!" Naomi shouted, pushing her head into the gap in the fuselage. She got no reply. If Skip was offline and her parents weren't answering...What if... She shook her head. "Mom!"

"If they're up on the bridge, they wouldn't hear you," Jax offered.

"Jackson, Naomi, Kori."

The trio spun around.

Baxter, Marshall, Steve, and Rogers were standing under the *Osprey*'s drive section.

"Baxter!" Jax shouted. He spied the droid's damaged body and the unconscious Chen in his arms. "You look bad."

"I have been better," the droid admitted. He tilted his head. "So has Chen."

"Is your med bay intact?" Rogers asked.

Jax shrugged. "Just got here." He waved a hand toward the ship. "Cargo hatch is fucked."

"Take him," Baxter said, holding out Chen's limp form.

Rogers nodded and accepted his colleague's weight with ease.

"The release is..." Jax looked around. He pointed. "There." Both large cargo doors had an emergency release control on the outer hull. Jax had never used them before. After a minute of fussing with the panel, he exposed the mechanism. Glancing over his shoulder, he said, "I'm not sure this will work with the door half off —"

The sound of wrenching metal cut him off.

Baxter lifted the thick, no-longer-straight piece of hull. With only the slightest sound of struggling servomotors, he tossed the cargo hatch aside. It landed with a thud.

Jax stared at his friend, mouth hanging open. He knew the ship was in awful shape, maybe totaled, but the casualness of tossing the cargo door was like a blow to the chest.

Baxter motioned Rogers in and pointed toward the aft section. He looked at Jax. "What?"

"Nothing. Let's go." He was quickly losing the battle against the tears that were threatening to burst from his eyes. The *Osprey* and Skip had been a part of his life for as long as he could remember. The ship had been his first home. Before the war, his parents ran cargo and the occasional security patrol for Kelso station, letting young Jax sit on the command console to see out through the transparent titanium windows.

Seeing her like this—broken, riddled with holes—broke his soul. He realized he couldn't hear the reactor. The ship's heart was cold.

"Commander. I'm not detecting any more cargo shuttles," a junior officer at one of the *Goliath*'s sensor consoles announced.

"Are they still jamming comms?" the leader of the Resistance asked.

"Affirmative, sir," one of the communications officers answered.

Everyone on the massive ship's bridge that didn't have something else to do watched as the last cargo shuttle, presumably full of droids meant to masquerade as shock troopers, came to a stop in the *Resolute*'s landing bay. The distance was too great for any detail, but the number of cargo shuttles landing was all the proof they needed that they'd lost.

Commander Roberts turned to his executive officer. "Status report?"

She turned from the workstation she was looking at. "Damage crews report that most of the hull breaches are patched or that they've sealed off the impacted sections. We're as airtight as we're gonna get without a space dock."

He nodded. "Weapons?"

Her face told him all he needed to know, but she answered, "Forward missile batteries are back online. Starboard point defense turrets are still mostly offline. Port side is in slightly better condition, but not by much. Our big guns, those still intact, are still offline."

The Commander swore and turned back to the main display screen. The *Resolute* and her surviving support ships were turning about, making ready to leave the system. Or were they?

"What're they doing?"

The *Hammer* wasn't turning to depart the system. She was moving closer to Gael.

"I think she's moving to a lower orbit," Lieutenant Vale said. She was watching just as intently, unsure what the Imperials were up to.

The *Goliath* and her small fleet of support ships were a light hour from the planet, watching via sensors while they made repairs. That the *Hammer*'s commanding officer hadn't chased them down was still a shock. Maybe they wanted the Resistance to watch what was about to happen.

"I think they're going to bombard the planet," someone said.

Roberts squinted at the screen. "Shit." He turned to his XO. She shook her head. There was nothing they could do.

The *Goliath* was in no shape to go head-to-head with the *Hammer*.

The interior of the *Osprey* was a wreck. Deck plating had buckled and there were half meter diameter holes burned through from cargo deck to the spaces above. The crash ripped the armory door almost completely off its hinges. The contents of the forward space littered the cargo hold. Small fires were burning all around, the smoke finding the holes between the cargo and common decks.

"Skip?" Jax called out again. No answer.

The med bay was in okay shape, all things considered. The auto-doc ran on its own battery. After Rogers eased Chen's unconscious form onto the bed, the spiderlike machine came to life, beeping happily as it scanned its patient. The diagnostic display was cracked and filled with static and artifact pixels. Baxter would have to act as translator.

Naomi, impatient to find her parents, said, "I'm going up." Jax and Kori nodded, the former turning to the Delphinos and Rogers. "Stay here. Just in case anyone gets nosy." He pointed to the opening where the cargo hatch had been.

The spiral staircase that connected the *Osprey*'s decks was more or less intact. It had come apart from the floor of the cargo deck, but after a short jump was still usable. Barely.

"Careful," Kori admonished from below Naomi. The handrail had broken free in several places, leaving jagged metal.

The common deck was in far worse shape than the cargo deck below. Blaster bolts from the antiaircraft battery had ripped through the ship, incinerating the sofa and over-stuffed chair that Jax's parents purchased when they got the Osprey. The bulkhead-mounted entertainment screen was a melted glob fused to the bulkhead. Some of it had fused with Rudy's recharging base.

"Damn," Naomi whispered.

Jax made a slow spin, taking in the remains of the lounge and kitchen area. It was a total loss.

Kori stepped up to him, draping an arm around his shoulder. "It'll be okay." She whispered, reaching up to stroke his sweaty, sticky hair. "You'll see." She gave him a reassuring pat on the shoulder and headed aft to take a look at the crew berths.

He sniffed, nodding. After a beat, he pointed to the top of the staircase. "Emergency seal. They've gotta be up there."

Naomi's gaze followed his gesture. The spiral staircase ended at what looked like a thick seal, closing off the circular opening between decks. It looked securely closed.

Kori came from the aft corridor, brushing her hands on her pant legs. Jax turned, a question on his face. She shook her head. "Not great."

Naomi climbed the stairs, reaching the thick emergency seal. She looked down at Jax. "Where's the release?"

Jax hummed. "Good question."

"It is on the bridge," Baxter said, his voice still more static than not, as he came up the stairs to the common deck.

"Can you tell if they're up there?" Naomi asked.

Baxter nodded. "Yes. I am detecting two lifeforms and

Rudy." He moved to the top of the stairs and wrapped his fist on the thick seal.

Rudy, we are here, he transmitted.

Great. We are trapped, and something is burning. The Himuras are struggling to breathe, the small navigation droid replied.

Baxter turned to look at the others. "The bridge is filling with smoke."

Naomi gasped.

Jax turned to Kori. "There's a pry bar down in engineering. Mounted to the bulkhead just inside the door!"

She nodded and turned to the stairs.

Naomi scowled at him. "That you remember clearly, but not where the release is?"

He shrugged.

Baxter reached up, trying to wedge his fingertips into the hatch's seam. It was no use. The emergency seals were designed to be as resistant as possible to being forced open.

Rogers came up the stairs from the cargo deck. "Everything okay? Kori sped by."

Jax inclined his head. Rogers looked straight up at the emergency seal. "Shit."

"Yeah."

Baxter slammed a fist against the hatch in frustration. If only his chain blades were intact.

Jax asked. "How's your pal?"

"Your auto-doc is a bit quirky but thinks he'll make it." He looked at Baxter. "Thank you for translating."

From the top of the staircase Baxter nodded, then said, "While I work on this, someone should check the computer bay."

Jax looked around. "I'll go."

Kori burst up through the opening in the deck, a thick

metal pry bar clutched in both hands. "This thing is heavy! Why did you send me to get it?" she panted.

Rogers took the heavy metal bar from her and joined Baxter at the top of the stairs. He slammed the pry bar into the seam with a loud clang.

Jax tapped Kori's shoulder and headed down the stairs. She fell in behind him as the sound of metal groaning filled the remains of the common deck.

"Think Skip is okay?" Kori asked as they passed the med bay. Chen was still unconscious on the table, the auto-doc clicking and whirring as it ministered aid.

"I hope so," Jax said. The entry to engineering was in shambles. The aft section hadn't taken as much damage as the rest of the ship, but the crash still did plenty of damage.

The door was open from Kori's previous visit. Walking in, Jax was impressed she'd found the pry bar as quickly as she had. The space was a shambles.

The ship's main processing cores occupied a rack along the starboard bulkhead. A clear security barrier, normally locked to the rack, stood shattered, hanging open. Normally, there would be hundreds of blinking lights. Right now, there was only one, a pulsing blue glow on what Jax knew was the main core. It was in low power standby mode. That was good news, as far as things went. Skip wasn't dead.

CHAPTER 18

On the *Osprey*'s bridge, someone moaned. Sparks rained from several conduits that had ripped from the ceiling. Flickering red light woke Kana Himura.

"Ow," she groaned.

Rudy, still clutching the console on either side of the Himura, beeped. "Are you two okay?" Wirelessly he sent, *Skip?* There was no reply. *Skip, are you online?*

"I think we're okay, Rudy," Hikaru said. His voice was weak, but Rudy's scans showed both humans were more or less unharmed. He released his grip on the console, leaving matching indentations where his hands had been. He helped Hikaru stand.

Smoke was filling the bridge. Rudy's head made a full rotation. Something under a panel near Jax's pilot station was burning. Rudy noticed that the chair with the welded-on cup holder was askew.

Kana grunted and cough. "It's jammed. The mechanism." She coughed again, pulling at her restraints.

Her husband rushed back to her side, tugging on the straps. The smoke was getting thicker.

Rudy pulled Hikaru away. "There is a manual release and actuator to the right of the emergency seal. You must get it open." He pointed toward the circular hatch in the floor.

Hikaru glanced at his wife, nodded, and headed aft.

A panel on Rudy's tube-shaped body slid open to reveal something that looked like a cross between a machete and a steak knife. Reaching in, he slid his fingers into the specially designed hilt. Not as good as blades built into his arms, but better than actual kitchen implements.

The smoke was filling the bridge quickly. Rudy could hear Hikaru coughing. He turned to Kana. "Please remain still." In two quick motions, he slashed through the seat restraints, freeing Kana.

She slid out of the seat to the ground in a coughing fit. Rudy slid his knife back into its special compartment on his way to joining the other Himura. "Have you found it?"

After a grunt, the older man said, "Yes, but it's jammed." He gestured to the mechanism in the floor, then slipped into a coughing fit.

Rudy pulled on the release handle. It didn't budge. "Not good."

"Is there another way out?" Himura asked. The smoke was low enough now. He couldn't stand up.

"No," Rudy answered. He turned a slow circle, taking in the small bridge. With the emergency shutters deployed, breaking the transparent titanium windows was out. Not that it was remotely possible for Rudy to break them in the first place.

Something below them on the common deck banged against the emergency hatch. The two humans jerked at the sound. Rudy held up both hands. "It is Baxter and the others. They are attempting to free us."

"They're going to bombard the planet!" another of the *Goliath*'s crew exclaimed. All eyes were on the massive Adjudicator class warship slowly dropping into orbit over Gael. The *Hammer* was not in much better shape than the *Goliath* but had the benefit of three cruisers and two frigates standing off nearby for cover.

The battle had not gone how Commander Roberts had hoped. The Resistance had more ships, not many, but probably enough to drive the Imperials from Gael, but they weren't close by, and losing them would be disastrous if things didn't go in their favor.

For that matter, losing the *Goliath* would be a major blow to the movement, which was why he'd issued the order to fall back. The massive warship had taken a lot of damage.

Which meant that he and the crew of the *Goliath* were about to watch the colony world of Gael be wiped out for nothing more than being vocal about their dislike of the Empire—a step the Emperor had never taken until now.

"They'll be in optimal orbital bombardment position in one minute," a crewer announced from a station in the back of the spacious command bridge.

Another added, "They're targeting the planet."

The huge mushroom-shaped vessel bristled with weapons of all types. Most of them were on the forward-facing side of the large mushroom cap-shaped primary hull. However, for planetary assaults and broadsides, hundreds of weapon bays lined the kilometer-long secondary hull. All of them were open, weapons protruding like spines: heavy plasma cannons that would rain super charged plasma down on the planet below, missile batteries likely loaded with nukes, and everything in between.

The rumor was that a single Adjudicator class warship could glass a planet in under two hours. If something didn't change, the crew of the *Goliath* was about to find out. So was the population of Gael.

Roberts swore. He hadn't heard from Rogers since the team went underground into the lab complex. He liked the Caruso kid and his colleague. If pushed, he'd admit to liking the other two, the brothers, as well. Well-meaning kids, all of them, even if Jackson pretended to not care about anything other than himself.

He shook his head. They'd lost their starfighters. The last report from Chen's forces was that some locals had arrived as some type of mounted cavalry. They had heard nothing since. Nothing more had been reported from the ground team.

The ceiling speakers, the few that were still working, crackled. "He-hell-hello. Is anyone there?"

"Skip!" Naomi exclaimed. She had been sure the ship's managing SI had been destroyed.

Over the sound of Rogers and Baxter straining against the emergency hatch separating the common deck from the bridge, Skip said, "Naomi? Hello. I am not operating at optimal levels right now."

She smiled. "I'm just glad you're functioning. Can you open the bridge emergency bulkhead? My parents are trapped up there."

"Working."

"Almost...got it," Rogers grunted, pulling the pry bar as hard as he could.

Baxter slipped his fingers into the gap. "I have it."

Rogers eased the pry bar further into the gap that Baxter was struggling to hold open. He jammed the bar up through the gap, pulling it toward him.

"Emergency bulkhead disengaging," Skip announced.

The heavy-duty hatch slid apart with a grinding noise, stopping at the halfway point.

"Warning. Emergency bulkhead da-dam-damaged," Skip said. His voice was flat, devoid of his usual personality.

"Mom! Dad!" Naomi shouted.

"Omi?" her mother called back before slipping into a coughing fit.

The two elderly Himuras poked their heads over the edge of the hatch, looking down. Rudy leaned over to do the same. He waved. "hello."

"Thank God!" Naomi breathed.

Baxter and Rogers helped Hikaru and Kana down onto the stairwell. Naomi met them halfway, pulling them into an awkward hug before ushering them the rest of the way down the damaged staircase. Baxter grabbed Rudy and headed down the stairs after Rogers.

Jax and Kori came up from the cargo deck in time to see the joyful reunion, each smiling. Once the three Himuras stepped off the stairs, Rogers followed. Baxter, Rudy cradled in his arms, came last.

"You look like shit," Rudy said as his big friend lowered him to the deck. The central column that the staircase circled—Rudy's usual mode of transport between decks—was bent in several places.

"I feel like shit," Baxter confirmed.

Once everyone was safely on the same deck, Jax asked, "What now?"

Outside of the ship, a low wail sounded. The sound pulsed, rising in pitch, then dropping, repeating.

Rogers swore. "I think take cover might be next. Those are civil emergency sirens."

"We lost. Can't they fucking let it be?" Marshall said as he threw both arms up into the air.

"Wait," Naomi said. She looked up at the ceiling. "Skip, is your long range comm suite online?"

"One moment, Nay-Niay-Naomi."

Jax looked at Kori, his worry clear on his face. She put an arm around his shoulder.

The ship's managing SI said, "Y-yes. Long range comms are available. Who-who would you like me to call?"

"The *Gol*—" Rogers started, but a slashing gesture from Naomi cut him off.

She said, "Wide band, all frequencies. The phrase, 'Gotcha fuckheads eight-zero-zero-eight-one-three-five.'"

"Rather ru-rude messa—" the SI started.

"Send it! Now!" she shouted.

"Transmitting."

Everyone looked at Naomi, who didn't stop looking at the ceiling. While the others had been trading blaster fire and quips with the Imperial technicians in the underground facility, she'd found the network programming interface for the hundreds of blank shock droids in the warehouse.

Aboard the INV-1217 *Hammer*, Captain Lucy Scanlon was watching as the first bolts of fiery death rained down on

Gael. Each red-orange ball would incinerate a half kilometer and super heat the atmosphere, causing further death and destruction.

For the last hour, unmarked cargo containers had been arriving from the surface, her gunners keeping their weapons' fire from them.

A bright flash preceded a rising mushroom cloud where a small oceanside resort town had been moments before. Scanlon smiled. "Imperial justice," she murmured.

Deep inside the ship in one of her multiple massive cargo holds, Lieutenant Kaneshiro heard the first thud.

"Hello?" he called out. No one answered. He headed in the direction the sound came from.

Another loud thud. Closer now.

Kaneshiro moved between cargo modules. He did not know what was in them; they were all unmarked, and he'd received no cargo manifests. He threaded his way between two modules toward where he thought the noise was coming from.

"Hello?" He rested a hand on the container nearest him. The thud sounded again, and he felt it. Something in this container was moving, throwing itself against the side.

He moved to the front of the container to check the control panel. Still locked. "Is someone in there?" He leaned his head against the thick metal door to listen. Something was definitely moving around in there. A loud thud forced him to jump back.

"I better call this in," he mumbled to himself. He took

another step back, tapping his comm unit. "This is Lieutenant—"

Both doors of the cargo container flew open, their hinges bent out of shape. Kaneshiro stumbled backward as row after row of mechanical skeletons stepped out of the container.

"What the—" Kaneshiro stammered. The leading shock droid lunged at him, silencing the scream he was about to release.

Every other container in the cargo hold burst open, spilling dozens of droids, all bent on one thing: destroying as much as they could. In every cargo hold that received the cargo modules from the planet, the same thing was happening.

Up on the bridge, an ensign turned from his station. "Commander, sir?"

Scanlon turned first. "Yes?" Her XO turned with her.

The young man swallowed. "Uh. I'm seeing system failures and malfunctions across multiple decks."

Commander Beaumont frowned. "Explain, Ensign."

Another deep swallow as a flush crept up the young officer's cheeks. "Several primary and secondary systems across multiple decks are offline."

"Why?"

"I don't, uh...I don't know. The systems are unrelated. Several even span more than one deck, which shouldn't," he spotted the look the ship's XO was giving him and stuttered, "e-even be possible."

Commander Beaumont rubbed his chin. He pointed to

the terrified ensign. "Get a team together and go check it out."

The young officer leaped to his feet. "Yes, sir!" He was off the bridge before Beaumont even turned back to Scanlon.

The ship shuddered, and several auxiliary stations went dark.

Captain Scanlon spun. "Status report!"

Beaumont was already sprinting across the bridge to the systems officer's station. He turned to look at the Captain. "More systems." He turned back to the station as the ship rocked. "Hull breach, Deck 12!"

"Explosion in Weapon Storage Bay 3!" another officer called out.

Hundreds of shock droids were spilling out into the *Hammer*'s corridors. They all had one directive: destroy everything they could.

Aboard the *Goliath*, one of the communications officers looked up from her console, her cybernetic right hand coming to her ear. "Sir, someone is transmitting a message on all frequencies."

Commander Rogers turned. "From where?"

"The planet."

He turned to the main screen, watching as the *Hammer* systematically bombarded the planet as she traversed her orbit. He sighed. "The message?"

The officer cleared her throat. "Uh, the message reads, 'Gotcha fuckheads.' Followed by a rather immature string of numbers." Her cheeks were bright red.

Rogers turned to the young woman. "What's that?"

She nodded. "Yes, sir." She slid her chair a few inches to make room for the commander to see the message.

He started towards the comm officer's station, then stopped when someone screamed. "Commander, look!" his XO shouted, pointing to the wide display screen.

The *Hammer*'s weapons stopped firing. Without warning, a section of the ship's secondary hull bulged outward before erupting briefly in flame. Debris spewed from the gaping wound in the ship's side as the flame suffocated.

Before anyone on the *Goliath* could say or do anything, another section of the ship exploded.

"Sir!" the senior sensor operator called out. "I'm picking up significant power fluctuations throughout the *Hammer*'s secondary hull."

"From what?" Roberts couldn't tear his eyes from the screen.

"Unknown, sir."

In truth, Commander Roberts didn't give a rat's ass what was causing the destruction aboard the *Hammer*. He turned to his XO. "Red alert. Battle stations."

The young lieutenant didn't blink before turning and barking orders to various bridge stations. The bridge lighting dimmed back to the red it had been an hour before. Overhead, speakers announced, "Red alert. General quarters."

Roberts didn't look away from the screen. "Helm. Take us in. Intercept course for the *Hammer*." He smiled. "Tactical. Lock whatever long-range weapons you've got left on those remaining support cruisers."

His executive officer turned. "Not the *Hammer*?"

Roberts shook his head. "Something seems to be taking

care of the *Hammer* for us. Let's make sure no Imperial ships leave this system." He grinned.

The bridge of the mighty warship *Goliath* snapped into combat mode, calling out acknowledgements and urging repair crews to focus on this or that weapon system. The ship's powerful engines spun up, a deep thrum echoing through every deck.

The fight, it appeared, wasn't over yet. Out the forward window, a dozen missiles streaked past on their way to the *Hammer*.

In the ruins of the *Osprey's* common deck, Jax shook his head. "That's what you were doing?"

Naomi nodded. "Yup. I couldn't make them self destruct or anything, so figured the next best thing was that they destroy whatever ship they were on." She shrugged. "Same result."

"No more shock droids," Kori said.

Naomi grinned. "Exactly."

Hikaru Himura coughed, his lungs still cluttered with the smoke he'd inhaled on the bridge. "That's my girl."

CHAPTER 19

The next morning, Jax and Kori watched as the heavy lift shuttle settled into a hover over the *Osprey*. The *Goliath* and her few remaining support ships had made quick work of the Imperial forces once the *Hammer* exploded.

It still wasn't clear if the ship died as a result of her captain issuing the self destruct order, or the bots that Naomi turned loose. Either way, the ship and the shock droids were no more, and that was all that mattered to Jax and the Resistance.

"Hate seeing her like this," Jax said, without turning to the *Osprey*.

Kori said nothing for a moment, watching a small army of the *Goliath*'s general-purpose bots work at securing the shuttle's thick cargo straps around and under the damaged Valerian Co-Op Infiltrator.

"I'm sure they can fix her," she offered.

Baxter approached from the building that led to the secret lab that was now mostly molten slag. "Those explosives sure did the job. There is not much left down there of any value."

Jax turned. "That was kinda the point."

The *Goliath*'s droids stepped back from the *Osprey* as the hovering shuttle retracted the straps, pulling the wounded ship off the ground. Clumps of grass tumbled from the ruined hole where a wing had been. The shuttle's engines roared as they took on the additional weight.

The combat droid inclined his head. After a few hours on the *Goliath* in the big ship's droid foundry, he looked and felt not as good as new, but better than he had. It would take another day or so for more substantial repairs to be affected. "Indeed."

Kori turned to Baxter. "Processing cores? The foundry? Got 'em all?"

"Yup. The Resistance techs are still poking around, but I did not detect anything, so doubt they will find anything useful. I think they just did not want to take a droid's word for it." He shrugged. "It was more slag than anything else."

"Good." Jax turned to his two friends. "I just wish we'd captured video or something. The Empire was planning to use droid shock troops to assert its power everywhere. People should know."

The cargo shuttle's lift engines strained further as it pulled the *Osprey* in snug against its lower hull. A loud clang announced the mating of the two vessels.

"You think they'd care?" Kori asked, her eyes flat and lips compressed into a thin line. "People have jobs. They see the Emperor's navy and shock troopers all over the place and feel safe. If someone else has to suffer for that, they're okay with it." She had finally heard from her colleagues on Jericho station. Their boss was in custody, several coworkers were dead. The rest, including her, were out of work. The Empire nationalized the station, and those businesses they didn't find value in were shut down or kicked off-station.

With a roar, the cargo shuttle rose into the sky, vanishing a minute later, on its way to the *Goliath*. Jax watched the shuttle depart, hand up to shield his eyes.

Jax shrugged. "Gael figured it out. Maybe word will spread?"

A personnel shuttle roared over the treetops, coming in to land nearby. He watched it settle to the ground. "Guess our ride is here."

The trip from the surface to the *Goliath* was uneventful. There was no longer an Imperial presence in the Boros system. The wreckage of the *Hammer* was still settling into a stable orbit along with two of the three cruisers that had escorted her. The surviving ships fled when the *Hammer* exploded.

Jax whistled as they passed the debris cloud. "Damn."

Looking over his shoulder out the shuttle's small window, Kori said, "Wonder how long this will last."

He shrugged. "Hard to say."

Standing behind them, Baxter said, "Before I departed the *Goliath*, its SI told me that they were relocating the entire Resistance fleet and operations to Gael."

"Guess they found a home then," Jax said.

Kori looked back out the window at the debris, resting a hand on his shoulder. "Hope the Gaels know what they're getting themselves into. If it wasn't for Naomi's," she wiggled her fingers in the air, "talent, this planet would be a smoking cinder."

Jax put a hand on hers. They watched the debris pass them by in silence.

The shuttle settled into one of the *Goliath*'s large hanger bays. Jax spied the Commander and Lieutenant Rogers standing with the Himuras and Delphinos just beyond the marked off landing area. In the bay's corner, the cargo shuttle was untethering from the *Osprey*.

The Commander stepped forward, offering his hand as Jax and Kori stepped out. "Mr. Caruso. Ms. Lightning."

"Commander Tight Pants." Jax shook the bigger man's hand.

Behind the Commander, Rogers raised an eyebrow, leaning forward.

The Commander extended a hand toward one of the landing bay's exits.

Marshall fell in next to Jax. "That tree is awesome!" he whispered.

Jax smiled, despite his mood. "Told you. Glad you got to see it."

Steve sidled up on Jax's other side. "How you doing, man?"

He pointed to the *Osprey* lying on the deck, tilted at an unnatural angle, resting on her belly. Her landing gear were still stowed.

Steve nodded his understanding. The *Buttercup* meant a lot to him and his brother, but nowhere near as much as that old Valerian Infiltrator meant to Jax.

Jax nodded toward the two Resistance men leading the group. "They're pretty sure they've got a few leads on infiltrators that they can part out to get the *Osprey* back in the air."

Steve nodded. "That's good. Right?"

Jax nodded. "How's the *Buttercup*, by the way?" He wasn't confident he could keep talking about the *Osprey* without tearing up.

Marshall clucked. "She's all right. They sent a crew down to get her back on her feet. She's too big to haul up here, at least easily. They're working on her planetside." He pulled out his gPhone to check the time. "They should be done in another day or two. Hope they fix the head."

Jax made a face. "You damaged the head when you crashed?"

Steve groaned. "No. He damaged the head after we had Indian on New Dallas." He pointed at Marshall.

"Oh yeah, it was—" Marshall started, but stopped when Jax held up a hand, shaking his head. He turned to Kori, who gave him a look.

A technician approached. "Excuse me." She looked at Steve and Marshall. "I wanted to run some ideas by you gentlemen. Since we've got your ship opened up, I wanted to discuss upgrade potential."

The two brothers exchanged a look and moved to join the woman. Steve looked over his shoulder. "We'll catch up." The trio headed off.

Watching them go, Kori said, "She's got two new best friends."

Rogers smiled. "Want to see the tree everyone's been talking about?"

Kori looked up to see his grin framed by slightly pink cheeks. "You flirting with me, big man?" His cheeks took on a red hue. "Show me your tree." She turned to Jax, Naomi, and the other two Himuras. "Catch up with you guys later." She winked and added, "Maybe much later."

Naomi shook her head.

Jax said, "That man has no idea what he's in for."

Naomi nodded. "Guess she and Marshall are for sure. No doubt. Over."

Jax shrugged. "Who knows?"

The Commander watched all of this with a sly smile on his face. He finally said, "Tour?"

The Commander took the others on a slow tour of the ship, avoiding the central concourse until the end. Roberts gestured to a table near the tree. He looked at each of them in turn before settling on Naomi. "Lieutenant Rogers tells me you've got some, well, special abilities?"

"That rat bastard," Naomi said under her breath. She met his gaze, holding her right arm out in front of her. Bio-circuits from her fingertips to shoulder and up her neck circled her eyes and pulsed with blue light.

The other man's eyes widened. "Incredible." He reached out to poke her arm, only to get a slap from her mother. "Sorry," he said, adding, "How do they work?"

Naomi spent the next two hours explaining how her implants worked to a rapt audience of her parents and the leader of the Resistance.

The Commander had his chin in his hands, sitting forward at the table. "All kids?"

"Yup."

He turned to her parents, who both said, "We didn't know." As one.

Naomi shook her head. "Something about our brains still being malleable enough to learn how the implants work at a basic level." She shrugged. "All in the past."

Jax smirked. "Don't get any grand ideas. She's my business partner. Not yours."

Roberts leaned back in his seat. "Still not on board with the cause, I see."

Jax shook his head. Though his resolve on the matter was weaker than ever before, he wasn't ready to admit that to anyone else, especially the leader of the Resistance.

Naomi glanced at Jax, then the Commander of the Resistance, shrugging.

The Commander returned the gesture. "Well, I should get ready for dinner." He turned to the elder Himuras. "I'll see you all at dinner?"

The pair nodded.

He turned to Jax and Naomi, who each nodded.

Over dinner that night in the Commander's mess, the conversation turned to what was next for everyone. The two elderly Himuras beamed as Hikaru said, "We'll be staying on with the Resistance."

Naomi, taking a sip of wine, nearly choked. After clearing her throat, she croaked, "Excuse me?" She had assumed her parents would be returning to Shise.

Kana smiled and patted her daughter's hand. "That's right dear. The Commander expressed an interest in our previous profession and since Shise is under more direct Imperial control, returning there doesn't make much sense." She turned to her husband, her other hand finding his. "So, here we are. Where we can do some good. Make up for some of the bad..."

Hikaru gave his daughter a small nod. "We can never make up for..." he coughed, "for what happened to you... what we did to you." His smile faded. "Maybe this is a way to make even small amends."

Naomi smiled, putting a hand on each of her parent's arms. She turned to Commander Roberts. "If they get hurt, I'll come for you."

The other man smiled and nodded his understanding.

Across the table, Marshall smiled. "How sweet."

His brother punched him in the arm. To the elder Himuras he said, "That's cool."

Naomi's gaze settled on him. "No. That is not cool." The smaller Delphino leaned back in his chair. She took a second, taking a sip of her wine. "It's fine. I'm fine." She looked at her parents. "I'm happy for you both."

Ignoring them, Kori turned to Commander Roberts and the two people to his right. "So, Commander. You think you can hold this system?"

The leader of the Resistance smiled. "We aim to try."

The large baldheaded man in a kilt to his right nodded. "Aye, and we'll make sure they have all the support we can muster." He turned to Baxter and winked.

"Bit bold, don't you think?" Steve asked. He scooped up a spoonful of peas.

The Commander nodded. "I think it's time to take our movement to the next level." He looked to the bald man, who'd identified himself at the beginning of dinner as Angus, leader of the Gael Resistance cell that came to Baxter and Lieutenant Chen's aide at the research complex. "We've got friends and I think it's time to call on them." He looked around the table. "Maybe having a place to defend will make a difference."

Turning to Jax, Roberts said, "Now that the Empire is down an Adjudicator and a few cruisers," he spread his arms wide, "well, it seems like now or never."

Jax whistled low and slow. "They do have more, you know...warships, I mean. Lots of them."

Roberts smiled. "Fewer than you might think." He took a sip of his wine, his smile lingering on his eyes.

"And the Resistance is not without friends," Rogers

added with a smile, nodding to the bald Gael at the other end of the table. He made a show of turning to Jax and his friends.

Kori cocked her head to the side. "Sounds like things are gonna get interesting around here."

Rogers locked eyes with Kori. "Only one way to find out."

Jax and the Delphinos looked from Kori to the big Resistance man and back, sharing a look.

"I see you," Kori growled.

The three men suddenly found their plates incredibly interesting.

Since repairs to the *Osprey* would take at least a few weeks, if not a month or more, Jax and Naomi hitched a ride home with the Delphinos aboard the *Buttercup*.

Rudy stayed aboard the *Goliath* to keep Skip company and ensure his processing cores were repaired correctly. Baxter insisted on staying with Jax. The big bot did not for one second believe his human friend would be okay on the Delphino brothers' ship. It looked like it was held together with tape and good intentions.

Without a job and looking to lie low, Kori stayed aboard the *Goliath*. The others made sure she knew they saw right through her reasoning. The blush on Rogers' cheeks as they departed was all the evidence they needed they were right. Naomi was happy for her.

"Your ship smells like ass," Jax whined. He and Naomi were sharing the small love seat in what passed for a lounge aboard the *Buttercup*. Despite the ugly old freighter being fifty percent larger than the *Osprey*, most of that space was cargo hold. The space dedicated to crew was considerably more intimate.

The lounge had a similar arrangement to that of the *Osprey*: a love seat and recliner made up the seating area, both facing a large entertainment display mounted to the far bulkhead.

"I thought the Resistance technicians made repairs," Naomi added.

"You're welcome to get out and walk," Steve replied without looking up from the tablet he was reading while sprawled out on the recliner. The Delphinos' ugly mid-size freighter was two days out from Kelso station.

Marshall walked in from the corridor that led to the crew berths. "Avoid the head for a while."

Naomi looked at Jax. "Maybe if we get out and push?"

Ignoring them, Marshall shoved his brother aside, taking his seat. "So..."

Naomi turned to the older Delphino. "I already told you. We're not having an orgy."

He scoffed. "Oh, come on! Two of us have already done it! We're fifty percent there!"

Steve, pulling out a stool from under the small island in the kitchenette, said, "Don't bring me into this...and also, ew."

Jax made a face. "Don't worry, no offense taken."

Marshall shrugged. "Anyway. You thought about what you're gonna do when you get back home? No *Osprey* for at least a few weeks..."

From the kitchenette, Steve said, "I heard closer to a month." He grinned at Jax. "Or more."

Jax met Steve's gaze and shrugged. "I'm sure something will come up." He grinned. "It always does."

The End

As they say, there's no harm in asking, so here we go.

If you can help connect me with someone who can get The Grand human Empire on a screen (Big or Little) I'll cut you in for 10% (Up to $10,000) of whatever advance is paid.

Send me an email and we can discuss.
rights@johnwilker.com

ACKNOWLEDGEMENTS

I couldn't do this without an amazing group of people who support me.

Thank you Beta readers!

- Rick Lindsay
- CJ Boyd
- Roger Gilmartin
- Scott Jann
- Felix Muller

And of course, my editor, Christina Short, keeps me sounding coherent. Thank you!

Thank you so much, all of you!

The Space Rogues Series. Wil Calder and a bunch of alien misfits somehow keep finding themselves in the thick of it. No one ever checks qualifications when it comes to saving the galaxy!

The Grand Human Empire Series. Jax, Naomi and the droids are just trying to get by. New droid parts ain't cheap after all.